MILES

The Mavericks, Book 07

Dale Mayer

MILES: THE MAVERICKS, BOOK 7
Beverly Dale Mayer
Valley Publishing Ltd.

ISBN-13: 978-1-773362-91-5
Print Edition

About This Book

What happens when the very men—trained to make the hard decisions—come up against the rules and regulations that hold them back from doing what needs to be done? They either stay and work within the constraints given to them or they walk away. Only now, for a select few, they have another option:

The Mavericks. A covert black ops team that steps up and break all the rules ... but gets the job done.

Welcome to a new military romance series by *USA Today* best-selling author Dale Mayer. A series where you meet new friends and just might get to meet old ones too in this raw and compelling look at the men who keep us safe every day from the darkness where they operate—and live—in the shadows ... until someone special helps them step into the light.

When his call came, the mission was the opposite of what he expected ...

Returning to his hometown of London, UK, was a happy surprise, until he realized what—and who—was involved. Out of his comfort zone when dealing with women sold into sexual slavery or even "collected," regardless Miles was determined to dig in deep, when he realized he knew the latest kidnapped victim. A woman who'd touched him years earlier. To think she might be suffering at the hands of a deranged serial kidnapper or, worse, could be sold in some human trafficking ring ...

Vanessa, tied up and blindfolded, has no idea why she'd been kidnapped. She does her best to obey her captor, even as she plots her escape. Her hope is that she's been reported missing and that the cops are looking for her. … They are, but so is someone else …

Keeping Vanessa safe at his side, Miles is taxed to the limit to unravel and to capture a serial killer who's lain undetected for decades, disguised as a serial kidnapper …

Sign up to be notified of all Dale's releases here!
https://geni.us/DaleNews

Books in This Series

Kerrick, Book 1

Griffin, Book 2

Jax, Book 3

Beau, Book 4

Asher, Book 5

Ryker, Book 6

Miles, Book 7

Nico, Book 8

Keane, Book 9

Lennox, Book 10

Gavin, Book 11

Shane, Book 12

Diesel, Book 13

Jerricho, Book 14

Killian, Book 15

Hatch, Book 16

Corbin, Book 17

Aiden, Book 18

Boxed Sets and Bundles

https://geni.us/Bundlepage

CHAPTER 1

MILES RADFORD POURED himself his first cup of coffee and stepped onto his tiny balcony. He was renting a studio apartment with a lopsided built-in desk and a small kitchenette just big enough for what he needed for the moment. It was also month-to-month as he figured out his life. He had a lot of good options but nothing necessarily had the same adrenaline-pulsing lifestyle that he was used to. Nobody who became a Navy SEAL ever considered what came afterward.

The average participation in the program was eight to ten years. He'd already done fourteen and was well past the point of moving on, but he couldn't stomach imagining himself as one of the brass behind a desk. He wasn't *past* anything. He preferred something much more subtle and more suited for him. He couldn't describe it in specific terms, but helping Ryker out had been part of it. Plus rewarding to Miles. It had been taxing, sure, and dangerous. But reaching the end of it and also witnessing Ryker's hell of a new beginning with Manila was a better way to say it. Miles hated to admit it, but he was almost looking for something like that himself. The same as a hell of a lot of other men too, apparently.

He'd heard of various lucky-in-love factions within the navy. Obviously he knew Mason and his team. And also

Levi, who'd set up Legendary Security, with his partner, Ice, who also had this incredible matchmaking system. Both men were leaders in their own right but would deny their matchmaker abilities until they were blue in the face, but something was magical about them.

And now something was magical about the Mavericks team. It wasn't their official name, but it had been coined and had stuck. They had a Mavericks chat window, aka the command central, and a growing number of members on the Mavericks team. But, so far, two men were assigned to a mission, and then the others worked in the background. Somehow they understood they were being tested and trained for something bigger.

Miles sometimes wondered if he even wanted bigger stuff. He had told Beta, his Mavericks contact, that he would consider another job if it came up. Having helped Ryker, Miles would now have his turn next to lead an op. If he wanted it. That was one of the things that he liked most about this. They were given a choice—unlike in the navy, where they had no choices.

It had always been *You're part of the team, so you'll do this for your country*, and he'd been happy to do so—until he got to the point where he wasn't quite so happy all of a sudden. He realized it when just waking up morning after morning became something he dreaded. He then wondered how much longer he could do this, and, at that point in time, he knew it was already past his time to leave the more rigid military setup.

Honestly Beta's call had come at the right time. Miles had gone out to help Ryker and, so far, hadn't looked back, but now there was this edginess and sense of waiting, this questioning of whether he took on his new offer. Of course instinctively he would, because he had never yet turned anybody down when they needed help. Especially if it was a serious breach of keeping the peace in this world.

He hated the fact that the world was such a mess and that teams like the Mavericks were required. They were simple, subtle and got the job done though, and he loved that part. He just didn't know what kind of job he would be sent on.

So far, they had been everywhere from Thailand and China to Alaska. England too. Kerrick had taken that first job. And now that he had thought about it, Miles wouldn't mind going back to England. It was his home country, after all. However, he hadn't lived there in a very long time.

When his first cup of coffee was done, he got up and poured another one, and heard his phone buzz beside him. He took his phone and his coffee out on the balcony to answer Beta's text.

Are you ready? Beta had asked.

Miles stared at it for a long heart-stopping moment. He'd just been thinking about this moment and now here it was. And still he knew without hesitation what his answer would be. **Yes. Where's the job?**

England.

He smiled at that. That's where he had wanted to go.

Good. What part?

London.

Okay. Traveling on my own?

Package is being delivered right now. Use the alias. Details are in the microdot.

Sunglasses?

Yes. Call us after you've read it.

Just then his doorbell rang. He hopped up and ran to the front door, then signed for the package from a delivery guy and walked back out onto his balcony. There, he quickly opened the envelope to see his alias was still Miles. Only his last name was now Ryker. *Miles Ryker?* A play on words? His real name was Miles Radford. But it was close enough that he wasn't likely to have a problem with it. A piece of double-sided tape held a tiny dot, and the sunglasses were inside too. He put on the glasses and fitted the microdot in the corner where the screw belonged and watched as the data flowed.

He poured himself a third cup of coffee and sat down before slowly studying the material as it moved across the lenses. He hadn't even checked his flight details, and that was something he should do immediately. But he was too absorbed in what was going on because this wasn't a normal case. This wasn't government. This was Interpol and MI6. But not a terrorist cell activity.

It was a serial kidnapper.

He shook his head at that. It was definitely not what he expected. Just then, a redhead flashed onto his screen. Creamy white skin and freckles high across her cheeks and nose rained over his field of view. She had emerald-green eyes.

He knew her. Not in the biblical sense. But in the sense of any man staring at his dream woman—even if completely out of his league or who would never walk into his normal everyday life. Her almost too-perfect face would cause anybody to wonder if this picture wasn't a CGI mock-up or an Avatar, so to speak. But over the years Miles had seen her unretouched paparazzi photos—that seemed intent on making these beautiful people appear less than beautiful— which made her so striking in real life, sans makeup.

And then read her name. Vanessa Redburn.

Yep, he knew her. Something about her had called to

him. From many years ago. Yeah, beautiful women were all over the world. Some pulled at him more so than others.

Then there had been Vanessa Redburn. She was his dream girl. Her face had adorned many a magazine and billboard. Hard to miss anyone so spectacular. He laughed as he mentally reviewed the women he had dated over his life. He shook his head. He had unknowingly but always compared them to Vanessa Redburn. Unfair, yes. But that had been his ultimate bar to reach.

No wonder he remained single. He had blamed his career. It took a special woman to hook up with a Navy SEAL and not let the worry about the dangers of his job eat away at their relationship.

Aside from Vanessa's beauty, Miles wondered about the real test: Was she genuine? Was she good-hearted? Was she honorable, trustworthy, a kind soul?

He would find out shortly.

In his lovestruck mind, she was always just *Vanessa*.

But now he had to extract himself from his intrinsic tie to this woman to a strictly mission-related purpose, so he studied her last name. Now that made a lot of sense. Redheads were notorious for their tempers. And also notorious for not being able to handle much pain and much sun. He studied her features closely, analytically, from a facial recognition viewpoint, and memorized as many details as he could, right down to a slightly larger freckle just below the corner of her right eye.

With this case and the horrifying endings already circulating his mind, he suspected he would have to find this freckle to confirm it was her. He swallowed and reminded himself this was the job.

As he kept reading, the notes came in. *The woman didn't*

show up for work this morning. He checked his watch. It was seven o'clock his time, which meant it was three p.m. in England. Almost the end of the workday depending on what shifts anybody worked. *Model. Photographer. Author.* He shrugged at that. He could imagine her in that field with her striking looks. Apparently she was due at a photo shoot and one that was very dear to her heart as an animal activist in the protection of foxes. Foxes in England? That would never go down well.

Miles read more information, but the data on her location of abduction was very lacking. Nobody knew anything about what happened to her or why. It was assumed she'd gone out for coffee and then lunch with an old friend and that she blew off the photo shoot or had completely forgotten. But then the next line stated, *She's never done this before and had never been expected to be the person to do this.* He reread that sentence, hoping against hope that Vanessa was somehow okay.

And that's when someone responded.

May we help you with something here?

His microdot was somehow connected to his Mavericks contact person or the chat window or whatever. Someone must have been watching him read over this file too, seeing which line he had just read. Amazed at the technology, he asked out loud, "How far away was the photo shoot from her apartment?"

Within walking distance. Flat has been searched, someone typed. **No sign of her. She doesn't own a vehicle.**

"Traffic cams?" he asked.

Nothing yet.

"How far from her place have you checked?"

Four point five blocks.

He frowned. "None of the traffic cams saw her there?"

Construction along the entire way.

He nodded. "And, of course, somebody chose that time to snatch her off the streets too."

Yes.

"Who called it in?"

Younger sister. There is only the two of them.

"When did she realize it was that serious?"

The photographer at the photo shoot got pissed off, but Vanessa also had a meeting planned with the photographer that afternoon. When Vanessa didn't show for that, the photographer came around to her flat, sure that Vanessa must have been laid up with the flu or passed out unconscious. She was that worried because it was so uncharacteristic.

Miles nodded slowly. "And found?"

Younger sister. Devastated that nobody had seen Vanessa. She immediately called Scotland Yard looking for answers.

Not the cops?

Sister is an artist and dating a PM's son.

"So, a few extra phone calls changed hands to bring this to the higher echelons, is that it?"

Yes. The fact is, Vanessa is very well-known, and this kidnapping is very high-profile.

"And yet it's hardly the kind of job that we do normally."

Normally.

But nothing else was added to that comment. Miles frowned, not sure how this communication-via-sunglasses system worked. But regardless, he now knew, from his reading so far of the microdot data, that a lot of fathers had called in reporting their daughters missing on previous cases, and unfortunately too many of those remained unsolved. Miles hoped that wasn't the case with Vanessa.

"And we have nothing further to go on?"

Her phone had a tracker, but it is no longer active.

He frowned. "That's not good."

You leave in one hour and forty-five minutes. Are you on the road?

"Not yet." He swore as he pulled out the rest of the items delivered to him and found his ticket. A cab was pulling up to the front of his building, and he swore again.

Always check the tickets first, the message read. **We'll contact you later.**

Miles pushed the sunglasses up onto his forehead, then grabbed his ready bag, which he repacked every time he returned home. He added a few shaving and personal hygiene items too and picked up his wallet. Then he did one last glance around, locked the door and headed to the cab. He was at the airport in twenty-five minutes and just barely made it through security and to his gate, where they were already preboarding his plane.

He was ushered into first-class immediately. He liked that. As soon as they were airborne, he brought the sunglasses back down over his eyes and went through the dossier again. He still had the envelope in his hand and his laptop with him. As soon as he opened up his laptop, he brought up the Mavericks chat window and asked for a download of the dossier. He was given instructions on how to do that.

Interestingly enough though, it downloaded onto his phone. But, from there, he could at least read it without wearing sunglasses inside an airplane. He pushed the sunglasses back onto his forehead and wondered how many other team members had had the glasses or if this was a new prototype. He asked about that in the chat window and got an answer that interested him.

No, we've developed the technology. Now you're getting the updated version.

Are they good for anything else?

You can always contact us this way.

Now that's helpful, he typed.

Yes. Very.

Immediately he asked the Mavericks chat window for information. **I want her last-known GPS location, the address of her apartment, a map showing the apartment in its surrounding area and the construction zone, as well as the location of the photo shoot and which traffic cams were down.**

On it.

And then, remembering what had happened last time, he typed, **Ryker, is that you?**

A happy face came back and a thumbs-up sign.

Damn, Miles typed, **am I glad to be in touch with you.**

The answer came back, **Ditto. You ready for this one?**

Not sure, he said. **Not sure I want to be alone on it either.**

You're not. Just keep moving forward. Your partner will show up.

You're not giving me a name, huh?

You'll know him when you see him, Ryker said. And then he signed off.

As Miles signed off, several links popped up. He opened them to see the traffic camera feed from the day. He saw a brief glimpse of the apartment which showed the corner facing the cameras. Miles thought he saw somebody walk by a window, and then a door opened, and the cameras went off. And, of course, it was right at the start of construction time, around thirty minutes past seven. Somebody somewhere seemed to realize the construction was due to start, so they flipped a switch, and the street cams were down. They didn't come back up for the rest of that day.

Miles swore softly, and the person in the seat next to him on the plane glanced over. Miles smiled and said, "You know what it's like when reports are incomplete."

The businessman rolled his eyes. "Yeah, I do," he said. "It's a pain in the ass. We pay these people, and all we get is half-assed jobs."

"Exactly." Still, he did a quick summary of the notes and went through all the other links. However, nothing was suspicious. Sighing and opening the chat box, he typed in his request, asking for the traffic cams for the two weeks prior that focused on her apartment building. It took less than a minute for him to have a link. Slowly he worked his way through those. It was a long flight to London anyway, so he had time.

He made it through an on-board meal with several cups of coffee, intent on finding something in the street cams before he slept for a few hours, to help him with jet lag. He may have left San Diego today about midmorning, but he would be landing in London midafternoon the next day, due to the eleven-hour flight added to the time zone change that jumped him ahead eight hours.

He had gone through a day and a half of videos prior to her disappearance before Miles recognized the same person twice. And, with that face stilled, Miles slowly zoomed in to see what he was looking at. A man, also a redhead, close enough in resemblance that Miles wondered if he was a family member heading up to Vanessa's apartment. The second time Miles caught sight of the same redheaded man, he didn't go into the apartment though. He just stood outside watching.

Miles took a screenshot and then a close-up on his face and sent them to the chat box. **Find this one.**

Ten minutes later the reply was **A cousin.**

And details were attached with his age, phone number and address. The cousin's address was about ten blocks away from Vanessa's apartment. Miles frowned at that, as he slowly closed his laptop, resting his eyes for a bit. The next thing he knew, the flight attendant was speaking to the passengers, notifying them to get ready to disembark. Then he laughed. *Disembarking.* It seemed like he'd spent his life traveling. But, as soon as he got into the airport and beyond, he knew somebody would be waiting for him.

Sure enough, he hadn't gotten more than five steps out into the bright sunlight when the massive swarm of people at the airport clogged up the space and his field of view. Some people's arrival drew their complete family to the airport. He gave a terse shake of his head and stepped around the large group, almost plowing into somebody right in front of him. He stopped and stared, and it took a moment to register who he stared at.

But, by then, the man had already thrown his arms around Miles's shoulders and gave him a hug.

"Dammit, Nico," Miles groaned. "Do you have to give huge hugs every time we see each other?"

Nico stepped back with a laugh. "It's my Greek heritage," he said. "You remember my mama? She'd never let you walk out of that house without a hug."

Miles laughed. "I have such great memories of your mom."

"Yes. She's still sorely missed," Nico said with a sad smile. "Come. Let's go."

And then Miles realized Nico was here for him, which meant Nico was part of the Mavericks. Miles studied his old friend, loving the sense of familiarity and the homesickness as soon as he had connected with him. They got into a small and sleek sports car. Miles's eyebrows shot up. "Wow. Nice car."

"You know me," Nico said. "I love my comforts."

"Yeah," Miles said slowly. "Does this mean you're part of the group?"

Nico slid him a sideways glance. "And again you know me. Anytime there's a sense of danger and action and a chance to be a hero, I'm right there."

"And what happened to your navy days?"

"Well, I left a good four or five years ago to join a special joint task force, but it was too much desk work," he said. "When this opportunity came, I couldn't resist."

"You were contacted privately?"

"I was, indeed," he said. "But I'm also here with the blessings of the British government, as I was working on a special job with them."

Miles chuckled. "Of course. They're hoping that you've come to help them out, aren't they?"

"Exactly," he said with an eye roll. "As if they don't know me by now."

"You still have to watch it though—still have to follow the rules. We can't have an international incident," Miles warned.

"I know. But it was too much bureaucracy and red tape, and all those lovely bosses who sit behind a desk don't know what it's like in the trenches."

"I hear you there," Miles said. "I believe you were briefed on this case?"

"Another reason why I was tagged. I was investigating the possibility of a serial kidnapper involvement."

"MI6 is interested?"

"MI6 is interested when it got a call from Scotland Yard. But I'd already been picking up on a series of missing redheads which I believe are all linked."

Miles stared at him and said, "I didn't get to the end of the dossier apparently."

Nico laughed. "They knew I'd fill you in as soon as I picked you up."

"So, fill me in," Miles said, swearing to himself. He hated being short on information. It's one of the biggest complaints he had had when he was in the navy. It seemed like somebody always knew something he didn't, and that really shaped a big part of how he worked. How was he supposed to do a job if he didn't have all the information he needed?

"Well, that's why they left it for me," Nico said. "It involved one of my cases too." So he launched into an explanation. "Seventeen redheads have gone missing in the last seventeen years. And I think they are all linked to one kidnapper."

Miles stared at him in shock. "Seventeen years and nobody was on this? Nobody found this guy?"

"Do you know how many times somebody has to go missing to see a pattern?" Nico asked. He drove fast through the traffic, switching lanes and hitting the roundabouts at a speed that only he would take. His uncle had been a race car driver, and so Nico had spent many a happy day on the tracks with him. But he was also the best and the safest driver

Miles had ever been with. He handed him his life on a platter many times when they've gone out driving. This was Nico's forte.

Why he hadn't gone into the race-car world though, Miles didn't know. When he'd asked, Nico laughed and said, "There wasn't enough excitement. Once you knew you were a winner on the track, where else did you go?"

And Miles understood that too. "So, it would have taken three to four or five years maybe for them to recognize a pattern, I guess, what with only one a year going missing."

"No, a lot longer because they weren't all taken from the same location or even the same city."

"Shit."

"Yeah."

"Any bodies shown up?"

At that, Nico shot him a look and shook his head. "None."

"How about unidentified crispy critters? Or any bodies missing heads and missing fingerprints?"

"None," Nico said. "But that definitely reveals your mind-set."

"No," Miles said. "I'm a team player. This is very much police detective work, and I feel very out of my element here."

"Well, it's because of who she is that we were brought in, and it's also because of who I am and what I was working on that I've been asked to help you out on this case," Nico said.

"I hate to think that it's because she's somebody more important than another redhead," Miles said slowly. He really didn't like that philosophy in life. Even with his special connection to Vanessa, he didn't like this particular kind of hierarchy.

"It's not that. It's a personal viewpoint," Nico said. "We also found photos in Vanessa's apartment of other redheads. One is her sister. And another one of them belongs to the prime minister's family."

"Shit."

"So MI6 is now involved too," Nico said in that ever-cheerful voice.

"As long as I don't have to deal with the bureaucracy," Miles said, "I don't give a shit who's involved."

"No, we won't be dealing with them, not directly. And certainly we're not reporting to them. Beta might have to, but we don't. We're the ones in the trenches. MI6 gets to deal with the fallout. But we have to find Vanessa, and we have to stop this guy. Right before he goes after any others on his list."

"Agreed." Miles had to keep his emotions in check and focus on the facts. "Did they all disappear at the same time of the year?"

"Yes."

"Are they all about the same age?"

Nico tossed his head back and forth as he mentally went through the ages of all the women. "Let's just say, they're all between eighteen and twenty-eight."

"And our latest woman is twenty-eight, so she's at the high end?"

"Yes."

"And they were all the same kind of redheads, meaning some particular hue of a redhead?"

"Yes, and no. Let's put it this way. All these women were of the orangey-red variety. But, more important, they were *all* natural redheads. And that is no small feat in today's world."

Miles whistled at that. "It's not as if our IDs state whether we are a natural redhead or not. Imagine asking any woman if her hair color was natural or from a bottle?" He laughed at that, needing a moment of levity here. "So, did a Peeping Tom check that out or what?"

"No way to know at this point, but keep that in mind."

"And unfortunately that brings up another nasty thought," Miles said, as he settled into the car, loving the race through town. He didn't know how the hell Nico didn't get tickets at every corner. "How many redheads did he take who weren't natural redheads and did they pay the ultimate price?"

This time Nico's gaze was hard. "My thoughts too. I tracked down any other missing women who I could confirm that fell into that category, and I came up with three more possibles."

"They all follow the same pattern?"

"If you mean that they all disappeared at the same time of the year and their bodies were never found, yes. My theory is that the kidnapper thought they were natural redheads when he first abducted them, but later he found out differently. So he disposed of those, I'm afraid, and went right out to get another true redhead for his yearly count. But we have no way to know anything beyond that."

Miles shook his head. "I presume this happened in his earlier years of this seventeen-year span and counting?"

"Yes, within the first five years, his learning curve. But I may have missed more of these women since this serial kidnapper is working from a lot of different locations."

Miles's irritation grew. "And where the hell is he disposing of the bodies where we may find those three possibles along with the sixteen from the prior years?" *Or seventeen.*

"He must have a killing field that no one has stumbled upon."

"Or," Miles added, swallowing, "has some horrific way of getting rid of the bodies." A picture of Vanessa immediately flashed through his head. *Please don't let this be happening.* "I hope I'm wrong here."

Nico nodded. "The problem we have is not enough info and too many theories. That's enough to drive anyone mad."

"Similarities between the women? School? Work? Education? Families? Chess club?" Then thinking of Kerrick's op, Miles added, "Mensa club?"

"No, no, no, no, no and no."

He stared at Nico. "So we're talking just a natural orangey redhead connection. There are thousands if not millions on this island alone."

"Thousands, for sure." Nico nodded. "A lot of redheads. Once it hit the news, they dyed their hair black though."

"That would make sense."

"Maybe, but we can't be sure that some of them haven't gone missing too."

"So, what you're saying is, we know of seventeen redheads who we're putting on this one kidnapper—plus your three rejected possibles—but we don't know for sure that he's not done more?"

"Exactly. It could be fifty for all we know. Maybe he kills redheads in the spring and blondes in the winter."

Miles stared out his passenger side window. "You know what? I'd rather take on a terrorist group than this, right?"

"I know," Nico said. "Something else I found I think had the Mavericks asking for you specifically for this job."

"So I have you to thank for this nightmare," Miles

joked.

"Yes. I came up with another theory, and I don't have very much to back it up yet," Nico said, "which is one of the reasons why nobody in MI5 would listen to me. Their focus is on domestic matters, not international crimes, like MI6. I think these women are being taken as part of a collection. Like people do with artwork or antiques."

"*Normal* people. But this nutcase has been supplying these redheads to somebody or somebodies? Instead of the actual kidnapper collecting them?"

"It's hard to say. But, yes, I'm afraid that's a strong possibility."

"Sure, but outside of it being a theory, do you have any reason to lean toward that theory versus any other?"

"A hunch. Granted, everybody's idea of beauty differs, like some art lovers gravitate to Monet's pastels but others like the darker Degas paintings. But these seventeen women are all beautiful, beyond that even. … It just struck a chord in me. And it could be our kidnapper's tell. But I know none of that is good enough to go on," Nico said. "So I'm sorry. Maybe not."

"Damn," Miles said. "I really don't like that idea. We've come up against the sex trade in a couple cases. Not that I've been personally involved, but I saw enough of it over in Thailand. I would just as soon never have to go over there again and deal with it."

"Well, my thought is they were keeping the women for a year, and then, after a year, they needed somebody new."

"And that could be the kidnapper or this purchaser?"

"Yes."

"You must have had something that triggered you into this line of thought."

"Yeah. A case a couple years ago of a group of men ordering up what they wanted for a weekend. They had them that weekend, and then the women were tossed back into the hands of the suppliers, and they were moved on to somebody else."

"But that's the way the sex trade is set up. Some guy says he wants a black-haired and blue-eyed twenty-five-year-old, and you know they'll give it to him, even if that woman has her hair dyed."

"I know," Nico said. "In this case, they found three women had been kept in his basement."

"Okay, that's nasty," Miles said. "How long had they been kept?"

"One week and they were all still alive."

"Well, that was a good ending."

"It sucks though how that shit happens."

"Because it still leaves us with too many theories and not enough data on our case of seventeen missing natural redheads, aged eighteen to twenty-eight."

"I know. That's why I'm here to help."

"Ha," Miles said. "Sounds like you're the one that I'm supposed to be helping."

"No," Nico said. "This is your case. We need fresh eyes on it."

"But it's a case and not a mission," Miles said helplessly. "You know this isn't my forte."

"But, in a way, it really is," Nico said. "Believe me. I had already talked to the bosses about a couple of the missions where we had to find who in our friendly teams were killing a lot of the prisoners out on our Desert Storm missions. You were the one who found the killer. None of the rest of us had a clue. That was all you."

"Maybe. But that's different from a serial kidnapper."

"Not at all. That guy killed thirty-two people. You're just confusing the issue as being a police matter versus some op, like what we're doing."

"Since when do black ops deal with serial kidnappers? Unless they think he's military."

"Exactly," Nico said. "That's where we are right now."

VANESSA REDBURN WOKE once again. Her senses were completely deprived. She had a bandage over her eyes, something over her ears, plus her hands were tied up and curled in on themselves. She laid in a fetal position, and she thought she had been in the same position the last time she woke up. In the darkness she had no perception of day and night, all her time running together in an endless loop. She didn't even know if she'd been here a day or if she'd been here several days. She'd been drugged, and her mind was foggy, and it was all she could do to keep her wits about her when she did resurface.

And then, as soon as she awoke, she fell back under again. Her current world held no joy. She had no answers, and she had no idea why she would be held captive.

She detested every single moment of this.

She had been walking on the way to her photo shoot, when, the next thing she knew, she was here. And that made no sense to her. But here she was. It was so much worse because of the sensory deprivation. Her mouth was parched, and, as much as she tried not to focus on it, the minute she tried *not* to focus on it made it ten times worse. She was desperate for a drink or anything to ease the parched sensation in her throat.

But the gag was just adding more fibers to her throat every time she took a breath. She'd given up trying to see because the blindfold was dark and impossible to see through. And every time she tried to open her eyes anyway, she came up against folds and folds of cloth that then hurt to close her eyes again.

With her ears blocked, muffled just enough that she couldn't really hear anything, she kept straining to hear regardless. She didn't even want to think about the pain at her wrists and her ankles, but it was there nonetheless. She was lying on a bed, and she could roll from side to side, but, since it didn't give her any advantage, she now lay quiet where she was.

She knew she had been shot several times in the arm with drugs because there was still a sore spot, and her brain was still fuzzy. But no words had been spoken to her. She heard no cries of anger or tears of sorrow. Nothing. Even now she didn't know if she was alone in this room or if other drugged women were here with her.

Just because she couldn't hear anybody didn't mean anything at this point. She couldn't quite grasp what had happened or why no explanation had been presented to her yet. As far as she knew, she had nobody who hated her. No competitor who would do something like this to take her off her perch as a model. It was a cutthroat business, but she honestly wasn't at the top.

She was working toward the release of her first nonfiction book on life and spirituality. How the hell was that anything that somebody would kidnap her for? Taking her out of the picture wouldn't stop the book from being published anyway. If anything, that would make the sales even crazier. How sad was that? She laid here in defeat.

Somebody had been with her maybe a few hours ago, but she dozed off again. Hell, it could have been yesterday, she was so disoriented. She also hadn't had a chance to empty her bladder, and that bothered her too, yet she didn't have to go—why not? She moved and felt something ever-so-slightly between her legs. That worried her as well.

Horrible thoughts filled her mind as she considered whether it was her cycle and maybe somebody had inserted a tampon to help her or was something much worse there? She didn't even want to think about such things. But there was definitely a piece of tubing, and, with that, she realized with horror that she likely had a catheter bag. Almost instantly her throat gagged as the bile of her stomach crawled up the back of her throat. When her gag reflex calmed down, she could feel hot tears at the corner of her eyes.

She didn't know what she was supposed to do and, therefore, hadn't tried to do anything. She didn't want to make her captor angry, whoever it was, but cooperating wasn't exactly getting her treated humanely, much less freeing her either. She had tried to loosen her wrist bindings, but that wasn't happening. Her ankles were the same thing. If only she could get something free and allow at least one of her senses to open up.

She rubbed against the pillow under her head ever-so-slightly. It scratched the side of her temple and dislodged the muff over her ear. Then she laid here frozen in place, afraid that somebody had heard her. But now, with one ear partially uncovered—but on the pillow side, so it was still muffled—she lifted her head and thought she could hear somebody. She froze once more, waiting for footsteps to come toward her. But there weren't any.

She felt more hot tears of frustration, anger and fear in the corner of her eyes, but she was pretty damn sure from the stained tracks on her cheeks and the tightness to her eyes that she'd already cried several times. Then what would anybody expect?

She didn't even know where she'd been taken from. She remembered getting out of her apartment and going down the front steps, and that was about it. She didn't think she'd had a chance to cross the street. She was only going a couple blocks. A path she'd taken many times though. But she hadn't made it.

She wondered if her photographer had put out the call yet that Vanessa had gone missing. She needed to be missing twenty-four hours before anybody would take her seriously. What a sad world it was that her life could end before that time frame was over.

As she thought about that, she crossed it off her mind because somebody had gone to great lengths to keep her alive. But then they weren't too worried about keeping her alive long-term apparently, as she hadn't been offered food or water. She shifted her arms once again and winced at a sharp pain in her shoulder. She frowned, considering it, and then wondered if she had an IV or a needle in her arm too.

Was she in the hospital? Or was she in some sort of a horrible lab and was now an experiment gone wrong?

Shudders rippled down her body as she thought about it. Just then she heard a loud *snick* of a door. And a voice. But she couldn't hear anything that was said. She tilted her head ever-so-slightly, trying to get an ear free enough so that she could hear more.

"She's alive. That's all you care about, so stop calling me. Just show up at our regularly scheduled time."

She frowned at that. He was on his phone. There was more discussion, and then the door closed again. But did the man step inside this room, or was he on the other side of the door, outside of this room? She felt certain that somebody was still at her side. She laid here quiet and incapable of doing anything.

When a hand landed on her shoulder, she gave a muffled shriek and jolted in place.

"It's a good thing you're lying there calm and quiet," the voice said. The hand clenched her shoulder but not kindly. "The girls who struggle have it much worse off."

Instinctively she knew that, but she didn't want to give him too much agreement in this. But she dared not turn around and try to kick him because she had no way to fight him off or to know if he had a weapon. She made an odd sound in the back of her throat.

"You thirsty?"

Immediately she nodded her head.

He laughed and said, "I'll give you a drink for being a good girl."

And the gag was taken off her mouth. It wasn't untied, but it was dropped down below her chin. She took several deep breaths, and a straw was placed in her mouth, and he said, "Now drink."

She sucked hard and fast, afraid he would take it away from her.

Finally, after taking in as much as she could, she stopped and whispered, "Thank you."

"No problem," he said carelessly. He took the straw away after she had yet one more drink and then put it on something close by, like a night table.

"Do I get any food?" she mumbled.

"Later," he said. "You might as well sleep now. It's the best way to pass the time."

"Time until what?"

"You'll see," he said. "Now shut up."

She fought against obeying his orders. She'd never been one who would lie down and take abuse easily. She was always the one who would stand up and kick out first, but this man … there was just something about him. Something painfully and excruciatingly indifferent in his mannerisms. "Why are you doing this?"

"It's what I do," he said. "If you keep talking, I'll put the gag back on." She fell silent in an instant, and he said, "Smart. I'll leave you like this for a little while, so you can calm down a bit. But, if you cause any trouble, the gag goes back on again."

"I can't cause any trouble," she said. "I've got no place to go and no way to get there."

"True enough," he said. And he walked away.

She heard a nearby door open again, and he called out something to somebody before closing the door again. But she wasn't quite sure. Somebody seemed to have arrived though, because he started talking again, but it was all distorted. Again she rubbed her head against the pillow a little bit to get that ear muff off. He was yelling now, so it helped her to hear better.

"Damn it, I just talked to him. Tell him that she's awake and cooperating."

"*Him?*" she whispered. "Who's him?"

More muffled discussions came, but then were gone, and then the door shut. And she knew that he was here with her again. She laid quiet then, not sure what was coming but knowing it couldn't be good. She hated the tears that even now worked their way out of the corner of her eyes. She was determined not to give him that sense of satisfaction, but there was nothing like being a victim. It took all the power away from her and made her cringe in a corner and accept whatever pain and punishment came her way. She couldn't let that happen.

But she knew that she would break just like every person would break under the right conditions. But she had so much to live for and so much to hope for.

And, at the top of that list, she was hoping for a rescue.

CHAPTER 2

HOPING FOR A rescue that didn't come was one of the most fruitless things, and yet something that Vanessa couldn't stop doing. Because, if she couldn't help herself, it was up to somebody else to come and help her. And yet, how could they if they didn't know she was missing?

He was still here beside her, silent.

She still had no gag on, and she was grateful because it allowed her to take deeper and easier breaths and to ask for water. The fact that she hadn't been asked if she needed a bathroom confirmed that she had a catheter. And the bag had been changed at least once. So, had she been here for twenty-four hours? Or longer? She had no clue.

"Food's here," the same voice said.

She smiled. "Thank you."

"I want you to sit up," he said.

The instructive tone of his made her feel like he'd given this order many times over. Her heart froze at that. How many other girls had he done this to? She struggled to sit up.

"Now swing your legs over to the side, so you're sitting on the edge of the bed, with your hands resting on your lap."

Again that same tone. It was bored. As if he didn't care if she listened or not. If she listened, fine. If she didn't, fine. She did as instructed, not wanting to see what would happen if she didn't, and a tray was placed on her thighs. She tried to figure out what was on the tray because her hands were still tied together. Her fingers could move, but it was hard to determine where to reach without her sight involved.

"You have two sandwiches," he said, "and an apple."

She found one sandwich and, in her mind's eye, worked her fingers down so she could find two sides of the bread and lift it up. And moving carefully, she brought it to her mouth. She knew that, with a lot of scientific experiments, people with their eyes blindfolded missed their mouth. So she made this move very slowly and touched the corner of her mouth with the sandwich and turned her head and bit down.

"Good. Look at that," he said. "You're one of the smarter ones." She ate while she listened to his ramblings. "The trouble with the smart ones is, they're too smart, and they think they can outsmart me. But it doesn't work that way."

She didn't dare say anything. But, of course, that would mean she was one of the smarter ones. Yet again, if she didn't say anything, he'd probably had many of them do that before too. She dropped her hands slowly to the tray, trying to find another sandwich. But her tray was empty.

He laughed. "If you want another sandwich, hold your hands out, palms up." She did as he asked, almost as if playing a game because he was so bored. But he gave her half a sandwich.

And when she put her hand on top of it again to lift it to her mouth, she found no top piece of bread. He laughed once more, but she didn't say anything. She just lifted it to her mouth and ate what he had given her. They went through that same process several times, but, each time, it was a bit different. Sometimes she was missing the bottom slice of bread to the sandwich, and the ham and cheese went directly on her skin. Sometimes she just got a piece of cheese.

She didn't care. She ate what he gave her.

When he was done with that game, he said, "Now you can have your apple." And he was bored once more. He got up and walked around the small room. "Jesus, I have to get out more."

She agreed but didn't say anything. She took a bite of the apple and winced. It was more wrinkled and mealy than fresh and crisp, but beggars couldn't be choosers. She finished the apple even though she was full because who knew when she would get another meal? As soon as she placed the core onto the tray, she heard him come closer, and he soon whisked away the tray.

He then told her, "Lie back down."

"Water?"

He sighed. "Yeah, you can have another drink. Hang on." He moved a chair back. Probably it's the one he had been sitting on—and placed the tray on top of it. She could hear the distinctive motions as he took two more steps, and she decided that the chair was probably about four feet in front of her. What were the chances she could jump forward, grab it and pound it over his head? And would that do any good? He might've already seen it coming or even had set it up as a trap, expecting her to try something like that.

Just then the straw was placed in her mouth. She reached up her hands, and he said, "Ah, ah, ah. Touch me, and I pull it away." She let her hands drop and accepted the drink.

"Good," he said. "That's what I like to see. Obedience. All women should learn obedience, but nobody teaches them that." He then took away the straw and put it on the night table with a hard *clank*.

She mentally measured that distance and realized that it was almost close enough for her to reach.

"Now," he said, "lie back down again."

Obediently she laid back down and shifted so she was farther over, not quite on the edge of the bed.

"It'll be a few hours before you get any visitors," he said, "so go to sleep."

"Visitors?"

"Yes," he said. And this time the bored tone was gone, and excitement was in his voice. "The buyer will be here. He'll check you over and see if you're okay or not. And you'd better be ..."

Buyer? At that thought of being checked over and having to pass inspection as to whether she was *okay or not*, the bile in her stomach rose again. She took several slow deep breaths and tried to calm back down again.

"If you throw up on the bed, I'm not cleaning it up. You'll have to lie in it."

As a threat, that was pretty effective. She laid here until she calmed her stomach again. As she did that, she pushed back slightly more of the earmuff covering her ear. Now it was almost all exposed, and, if there was anything to hear, she might be able to. She turned so she was partially on her back and partially on her side.

"Looks damn uncomfortable," he said, "but whatever. Like I said, sleep. I'll be back in a few hours." And, with that, he took several steps to the door, opened it and then closed it.

But, if she hadn't had her earmuff askew, she wouldn't have heard him still steadily breathing. She realized it was yet another trap. She laid with her hands on her belly and just stayed relaxed and calm.

After a few minutes, he murmured, "Smart girl."

And this time, he opened the door, stepped out and

closed the door. What she didn't know was whether he'd left anybody behind or how quickly he would come back or even if a camera was in here. She contemplated her options and realized what she really needed was to escape. But from where? If there was no window, how could she get out? And, if she was several floors up, how would she get down? She could probably use her hands to push her blindfold up a bit, depending on whether he was around and watching her or not and whether she'd get away with it.

Tentatively she reached her hands up and scratched her nose, then pretended to clean something from her teeth while checking if the gag was still hanging around her neck. When nobody seemed to be here, she pushed the blindfold up ever-so-slightly so she could see, only to find herself in a dark room with no lights. There was a window though, but only darkness greeted her outside. And, yeah, she was alone. It didn't mean no cameras were in here. It didn't mean she would stay alone. But she was for the moment.

As she rolled over again to consider the rest of the room, she was grateful to confirm being completely alone. Regardless of what he said about returning in a few hours, she didn't know when he would come back. As she sat up, she glanced at the bed and realized that the awkward pain really was from something inside her. She *had been* hooked up with a catheter bag, and it laid almost full between her legs.

MILES AND NICO were settled into a small apartment as their home base here in London. Miles was surprised because he'd been expecting a hotel room, but apparently they were using a safe house. He set up his electronics, but, in the back of his mind, he couldn't let go of the thought that this wasn't a military op. "And why would you think these missing redheads are military related?" he asked Nico.

"Again a hunch, but it also came from a serial killer we had exposed not too long ago," Nico said. "The serial killer was in the French militia. Anyway he'd been using his military missions to attack and kill women."

"Nice guy," Miles said, hating that anybody who had sworn to serve their country would be taking advantage of that to kill women. But then a serial killer or anybody of a mind-set to kill women in the first place wouldn't give a damn about loyalty to a country or using such an honor system as a shield. Obviously, from their point of view, it gave them the opportunity to travel and even some protection in most cases. "Are you thinking this is active military?"

"No," Nico said.

"You haven't got any bodies, and you've got no clue as to who's taking them or why the suspect could be in the military?"

Nico took a deep breath and said, "For basically those reasons, it's military precision—taking the women like clockwork each year, the cameras being down and the women never being seen again. We don't have a face to our kidnapper, so he's good at spotting cameras, and we don't have any physical description or other evidence to go by, so he's good at avoiding witnesses. He's stayed under the radar for a long time—that takes special skills."

"So, you are saying the skill set that allowed him to stay undetected and to find these women and to not leave a witness—or a body—behind to be found means he's trained? Because lots of serial killers were active for decades without that skill set. Just dumb luck as they honed their skill."

"That's what I was thinking. The counterargument is that, after seventeen years, he's got enough experience at what he's doing. Then he's good enough, but he doesn't have to be military."

"True. We have to keep an open mind, I guess. And, according to one of your theories, this woman's been taken already, and she would be the one for this year."

"Yes, but yet for some reason it doesn't feel like that," Nico said. "We also don't know if he'll change his pattern, but I can tell you that I'm getting a ton of pressure from the prime minister's family."

"You mean, now that their redheaded daughter might be targeted?" He tried to keep the caustic tone out of his voice, but it was hard. He didn't like the fact that, too often, the rich white families got all the attention, and any other nationality—with much less wealthy or less prominent families—*didn't.*

"I don't think it's that so much as now that we've finally gotten an added awareness on this and have realized there may be seventeen related cases that he's horror-stricken about it."

"Good," Miles said. "They should be horror-stricken. And it shouldn't have taken seventeen women to have gotten there."

"I know," Nico said. "Believe me. I worked this case and saw five of those faces on the board."

"And this is the sixth by MI6's count?"

"As of the time since I left, yes, it's the sixth by their count. We didn't find anything while I was in the department."

"So, any chances somebody in the division is involved?"

"Why would you think that?" Nico asked curiously. But

his tone held no shock, as if he'd already considered it.

Miles turned to study his old friend. "Because of the fact that no evidence has shown up, and we have nothing to go on. It always makes me wonder if somebody isn't removing evidence or burying it under a huge mass of other stuff."

"I did think of it," Nico admitted, "and I ran it through, investigated and interrogated the cops involved in all the cases, but I couldn't find anything. Absolutely nothing popped."

"Stranger abductions are the worst," Miles said.

"Spoken like a perfect detective comic-book hero," Nico said with a chuckle.

"Well, we need a hell of a lot more than just a handful of theories," Miles said. "I'm no Sherlock Holmes. We need real evidence to follow. There's got to be a trail of something."

"Well, I'm hoping your fresh eyes will handle that. You're the only one I know of who got through all that mess that we had on that military matter. Was that five years ago now?"

"Yeah," Miles said. "That wasn't a good part of my life."

"It wasn't a good part of anybody's life. Finding out one of our own had been killing prisoners of war to make it look like the other team had done it sucked."

Miles nodded. He tried to block out that case, but it was hard. He had been assigned to a joint mission in Iraq, but instead several prisoners they had found and had brought in were killed. And always made to look like some of the friendly team members of Iraqi soldiers had been the guilty party. Only through Miles's own efforts did he get to the bottom of it and found out one of their own had been behind it all. And, when the guilty party had been interrogated, he'd shrugged and said, "Well, what the hell? Why do we care? They're nobody. And we shouldn't be working with and friendly with these guys anyway. Somebody needed to see that they were dangerous."

And Miles had replied, "So, because they weren't dangerous Jihads, as you thought they should be, you made it look like they were killers?"

"Somebody had to. Jesus, Miles, since when are we out here shooting alongside these guys?"

"Every war has two sides," Miles had said quietly. "These guys were on our side."

"*This* time," his buddy had said. "Just *this* time. You know in the next kerfuffle, they could be on the opposite side."

Miles couldn't say anything about that because his buddy was right. It seemed like the friendly fire switched on a regular basis, and it made things difficult. Hell, it happened all the time with three siblings, where during childhood two would gang up against one for a time, then would regroup so another pair was against the remaining one. He shook his head. But this was worse. Far worse.

And to think something like that was going on here with these seventeen redheads … Well, Miles was pretty sure either somebody was helping this supposed serial kidnapper, or he was just that damn good.

And he also had a system to supply these very specific women. He had a network. But then people had to work for him. He couldn't have done all this on his own, and so Miles and Nico had to find the weak links in the kidnapper's system.

Why were these women picked, outside of their natural orangey-red hair and their youth and their looks, which already gave them enough specifics as to what made them a type? What was the kidnapper doing with them, and, if he was selling them, who was ordering these women? And, if he wasn't selling them, where was he keeping them? "If we could roust out a location where he was keeping these women," he muttered to himself, "that would help."

"No, that would blow the case wide open," Nico said. "Seriously, if we find the women, that's unbelievable."

Miles nodded. "I'm going back through the feeds on this latest kidnapping." And again he came up with the cousin. He brought over the files he had on the guy. "Any idea about what the relationship was like between the cousin and the two sisters?"

"Very friendly apparently," Nico said. "I interviewed him."

At that, Miles turned to look at him. "And how was he?"

"Nervous, upset and yet okay."

"When did you interview him?"

Nico flashed a sideways grin at him. "On the second-to-last case."

Miles bolted upright. "Seriously, the same guy I tagged on the most recent kidnapping case?"

"Not implicated," Nico corrected carefully. "Connected to two."

"But you're sure, absolutely sure, that he's not involved?"

"I would swear on my life that he isn't," Nico said. "But, like I said before, I'm too close to it, and I need clear eyes. So, you go over it, and you tell me if he's connected."

"Because, if he's connected, but he's not our guy," Miles said, "is somebody trying to make it look like he's our guy?"

Nico sat down heavily and said, "I wouldn't have thought so last year. Now his cousin has been taken. So now

I don't know."

"We need to talk to him," Miles said, standing and packing up his laptop. He looked over at Nico. "Have you got that interview setup?"

"I knew you'd ask," Nico said. He pulled out his phone and checked his calendar. "We have forty minutes to get there."

Miles rolled his eyes. "When were you going to tell me about that?"

"I bet myself how long before you would figure that out," he said, laughing. He walked to the door, and they undid the series of security locks and let themselves out.

AS THEY HEADED down the small back alleyway, Miles looked at him and said, "And what if I hadn't said anything about it?"

"I would owe me twenty bucks," he said on a laugh. "I would have then told you that we had him already lined up to talk to."

"Good," Miles said as they got into the car. "Has Vanessa's sister been taken into protective custody?"

Nico took a deep breath. "She refused to. Said that, even based on everything we knew so far, she was safe until next year."

Miles gave a half snort. "That's a lousy reason for not going into protective custody."

"Well, we tried to tell her that."

"But obviously you think she is in danger?"

"Yes, I think she is," Nico said. "I'm just not sure if it's for the same reason." And, on that cryptic note, he started the sports car and headed onto the main street.

"Meaning?" Miles asked after a while.

"She's within the right age range, but she's different enough that she wouldn't be the first choice of this kidnapper. She's more of a reddish-blond than a bright orangey redhead."

"Meaning, she doesn't fit the usual profile?"

"Yes, but, because the news has now picked it up, we'll get a lot of copycats. And what I don't want to see is her taken by somebody else who thinks, 'Hey, that's a great idea. Let's go kidnap a beautiful redhead woman and keep her chained up in my basement, and I can do whatever the hell I want with her thereafter,'" he said in a caustic voice.

"Did you explain that to her?"

"No. We're meeting her right after her cousin."

"And where are we interviewing them?"

He looked over at Nico, who smiled and said, "We have a room at the police station."

"Wow. And why the hell do I want to be there?"

"You're a special investigator. That's all you need to know."

"Shit," Miles said as he looked out the passenger side window. "I haven't had much to do with any of this. You do know that?"

"Not for the last five years but then beforehand you were bucking up against the military police pretty steadily."

"That's because I *knew*," he emphasized that last word, "somebody in our ranks was responsible. And I couldn't get anybody to listen to me."

"Because it was treasonous on your part to even mention it," Nico said quietly. "And nobody wanted to contemplate that possibility."

"I know," Miles said. "Believe me. It made my last few years that much more difficult."

Nico nodded. "It's also when I left. Remember?"

"And why specifically did you leave?"

"Because of somebody within our ranks," Nico said quietly. "Who the hell wants to work with guys turning around and pinning murders on somebody else? But it could just as easily have been the 'friendly' guys doing it to our team. And I decided I didn't want to live with that kind of betrayal anymore."

"Understood," Miles said. "And, for me, I had been dealing with so many young guys who, you just knew, when they started, were calling you grandpa and mocking you behind your back. And you gotta think, just maybe they don't trust you anymore."

"The young punks don't trust anybody coming in," Nico said. "They're full of piss and vinegar, thinking they own the world. They respect some elders to a certain extent—giving them their rightful kudos for having lived this long through all the shit—but, at some point in time, that respect wanes, even if you haven't done anything to get knocked down from that pedestal. The youths see themselves as the next wave of big cheese."

"Maybe they're right," Miles said. "We know that most SEALs don't last that long. The stress of the ops and the evil involved and the high levels they are expected to continually operate at is all incredible."

"You're one of the longest active SEALs," Nico said with a nod.

"*Was*," Miles said with a smile. "No longer active."

"Oh, you're active," Nico said. "You just don't realize how covert and specialized this Mavericks unit is."

"That's because we haven't been told jack shit about it," Miles said.

"And I doubt we will be," Nico said, "not fully, but I'm in because we have the scope to do so much more."

"Like finding a serial kidnapper on the streets of London?"

"I hope so. Regardless, we'll focus on Vanessa's case, on her kidnapping, on getting her back," Nico said. "Nothing else matters."

Miles thought about it and then nodded. "I've taken care of plenty of kidnap victims the world over. You're right. Our priority is not to get the kidnapper, but I'm all for that too. Yet our priority remains to get Vanessa back." As he sat here, he pondered about it and then nodded. "We haven't done enough research on this angle. Why her?"

"And you're thinking beyond the profile?"

"Have to," Miles said. "The thing is, she's also available. Too available. Just hit any of the social media sites and find where she was last spotted. Or check out her own website for an itinerary of her upcoming trips. People put too many of those personal details online for the whole wide world to see. She's a well-known face too. So either somebody was thinking that he wanted to add her to his collection or he thought that maybe it would be more of a challenge to take this one off the streets. Maybe he's bored in life and looking for more prominent people, for more risk, for more stakes?"

"Which makes the prime minister's family that much more of an issue."

"Sure," Miles said. "But we don't have a year's leeway to solve this. We've got to get Vanessa back in a few days."

"Faster, I hope," Nico said.

"I know. Otherwise she'll disappear into some underground system and possibly already has. And it'll be almost impossible to track her down. And we can't get hung up on the red hair because it could have been dyed while she's a prisoner. We'll never recognize her. ... Except for that slightly larger freckle just below the corner of her right eye."

Nico cleared his throat. "You got a thing for our victim already?"

Miles glared at Nico's usage of the word *victim* when it came to Vanessa. "You wanted fresh eyes? Well, you got them."

"It's okay, buddy," Nico said, then laughed. "The bigger they are, the harder they fall."

Miles shook his head, ignoring his partner. "We need facial recognition on the get-go."

"We've been running that software since we realized that she'd been taken," Nico said.

"And what about the sister and the cousin?"

"Do you want them followed?"

"I want to know every move either of them took since Vanessa disappeared," Miles said, as he stared out into the buildings that traveled past him at lightning speed. "It's way too easy to think that this guy's a pro. Maybe he is a pro. Maybe it's by experience. Maybe it's by training. But the fact of the matter is, so far, he hasn't been picked up. So we have to think out of the box."

"You were always good at that," Nico said. "Tell us what we need to do."

Miles thought about it for a long moment before speaking. "We need more information. *Much* more. I want every step of those two people's movements—the sister and the cousin." He pulled out his laptop, turned it on. "I want an around-the-clock watch on Vanessa's apartment, but I also want camera feeds from several weeks earlier, before the street construction, and I want to know the names of everybody in Vanessa's apartment building, plus a face for each of them." As he spoke, he typed into his chat window, asking for this information, and then he realized he had no internet. Thinking fast, he pulled the sunglasses from his pocket and put them on. It connected him to his operative.

"Ryker," Miles said, "I need information, and I need a lot of it." And he fired off his demands.

Nico laughed. "Now that's more like it," he said. "Let's hope we can narrow this window down to the last twenty-four hours."

"I hope Vanessa can stand up and fight for herself," Miles said. "The trouble is, she's likely drugged, locked up and completely incapable of doing anything."

"Most likely, yes, but that doesn't mean that she isn't doing what she can."

"Right." Miles closed his eyes and sent out a whisper into the ethers.

Vanessa, if you can hear me, hold on, sweetie. We're coming. Come hell or high water, I promise I'll find you.

CHAPTER 3

VANESSA COULDN'T HELP but wonder if anybody was looking for her. She was supposed to have meetings and the photo shoot, then return home to her sister. Her sister would have at least raised the alarm. If nothing else, her sister was a worrywart to begin with. She often warned Vanessa, like about a couple boyfriends she'd had in the past, telling her how they were nasty pieces of work who she should get away from. She almost always took her sister's advice too.

Was that what this was about? A disgruntled boyfriend? Could you get rid of somebody you didn't like by contacting someone online to do it? If somebody had done you wrong, could you turn around and have them taken care of? Even not so much a murder-for-hire but just pick them up and put them someplace where they'd have to suffer? She hated to think so, but, with everything she had heard that was going on in the Dark Web—a place that she didn't understand except that it was for hackers and the worst of the worst—she realized that, if people could dream up any atrocity, it could happen in reality, ready and available for the right amount of money.

She couldn't help but wonder if that's what this was. And *this* went past her realm of even contemplating such a thing.

Her blindfold remained up on her forehead so she could see. She had even picked up her catheter bag and hopped around the bedroom. She'd made it to the window and looked out, but, of course, it was dark outside still. Yet maybe dawn approached? She glanced around, in a hurry to see if she recognized a landmark. Yet she had more pressing matters to confirm, all before that man returned.

She determined that she was on the third floor with a concrete sidewalk down below. And now she had to wonder if she could even get out of here. She'd have to shatter the glass—or hope beyond hope that the windows would open—and she had a bedsheet, but it wouldn't take her very far down. So her best bet was to attack her kidnapper. But he would be expecting that. If he'd had other prisoners here, they surely had tried something. The longer she was here, the bolder she would have to get.

The catheter, however, was still a nasty-ass problem. She stared at it and winced. She'd had surgery before and remembered having a catheter then and how the nurse had removed it later. That's what Vanessa had to do now: remove it. But, if she did, she had no bathroom otherwise, and that was a concern too. Not a nice one but something that she had to consider. She still had the water on the night table, and the more she drank, the more that damn catheter bag filled up too. She'd remove it at the last moment, before she made her escape.

She had no weapons, but she had a night table. A chair. There was a plastic straw too, and, as she thought about it, she wondered if she could use it to poke his eye. She hated the bloodthirstiness of these thoughts, but, at this point in time, she was not changing her viewpoint. She would entertain bloodthirsty thoughts if they got her out of here.

She hadn't been able to untie her wrists or her ankles though. The knots were so very damn efficient and tight that she wondered what the hell they were called.

Just then the door opened, and she looked up to see her captor.

He laughed. "Feeling a little more comfortable, are you?"

"Not much," she said quietly. She studied him, but, with his black hat over his head and dark sunglasses, she didn't see a whole lot. He had a beard as well, but she knew that that could be shaved off or glued on as needed. And he wore a T-shirt, showing a ton of muscles underneath, so he's fit and a gym buff or somebody who worked out consistently. But something was regal about his bearing. Almost a military precision. "Do I get more food?"

He nodded. "You will but not just yet. I came in to make sure you're okay before our visitor arrives."

She winced and murmured, "That can't be good."

He laughed again. "Maybe not but, for you, it'll mean a change at the very least. Don't you want to see who cares?"

"Depends on why I've been brought here," she said. She kept trying to maintain her cool, but she wanted to lunge at him and claw his face apart. And, with her building rage, she might pull that off, but he looked like the kind who could bend her into a pretzel shape and snap her backbone without even breathing hard. She was five foot ten and 125 pounds. She was a lean model, and she didn't have a ton of muscle, and whatever strength she had would be crushed as easily as peanuts in a shell for this guy.

He saw her gaze tallying him up and nodded. "Sure, you could try going at me," he said. "Others have. But I can tell you right now, it won't do any good." He lifted one hand and punched it into the palm of his other hand. Immediately his biceps and triceps bounced up and down his arm.

"I'm not strong enough," she said with a nod. "But you still haven't told me anything about why I'm here." She rubbed her temple.

Then he laughed. "You couldn't even get the bands off."

She looked at them. "No, they're very tight. Same as on my ankles."

"I've had a couple women get free of them," he said with a sneer. "I had to perfect my bonds."

"A couple women?"

"Yep. Women. All kinds and sizes." But he said it with such a flippant manner that she didn't know if she could believe him or not.

"And this person who's coming to see me, are you selling me to him?" She hated to voice the thoughts in the back of her mind, but she didn't know how else to get answers.

His gaze sharpened. "Baby," he said, "depends if he likes what he sees."

"I was afraid of that," she said with a nod. Then she rotated her neck ever-so-slowly, trying to work out the kinks and the stress, but her jaw had locked down so much that, as she clenched her teeth together, it was damn-near impossible to loosen it up.

"Better look your prettiest," he said. "And you need to behave."

"Or else?" she asked, desperately trying to keep the defiance back but hearing a note of it enter anyway.

He narrowed his gaze. "A little bit of spirit is fine. Most guys like that. But don't even think that a lot of defiance will do you any good. I don't have a problem blackening your eyes or breaking your nose or slamming that jaw off-kilter. The buyer won't be terribly happy, but he'll understand.

Particularly if I'm tuning you up for his use."

At his words, all the color fled from her skin, and she nodded. "Like I said, I'm no match for you."

"Remember that," he said. "Now somebody's coming in to take that bag away. I can't have you like that when the buyer comes to check you over."

She swallowed. "Check me over?" And that grin of his made her skin crawl.

"Well, the guy has to see what he's buying, doesn't he?" And, with that, he stepped out and closed the door hard.

She swallowed and could feel the tears in her eyes. *Check her over.* That meant strip her down for some guy to view her like a piece of meat. Disgust once again rolled through her. But this time, the sense of having to do something, even if she died in the process, came with it. She didn't want to be here for some guy to paw her over like a product he was checking to see if good enough.

She immediately went to working on her ankles, getting one long foot and narrow ankle through one loop of her bindings. With that off, she got her other foot loose too. She quickly opened up the binding so that she had something to use for her own benefit now. And then, knowing it would hurt like shit, she positioned herself so she could remove her catheter. Taking a deep breath, she let her breath out and pulled the catheter straight out. She took several deep breaths afterward and then stood back up.

With it now in the sink, at least her bladder was empty, and she was capable of walking around freely, except for her damn hand bindings. She had to get them off too. Using the same trick that she'd used for her feet, she got one hand loose, then the next. Now she had a second tie to do something else with. She quickly went to work on the bed, tying her bindings to the frame, and then got one of the windows open. She only had the bed frame to tie her escape rope on.

She knotted the thin summer blanket, hoping it was long enough to at least get her down one of these three stories. And, with that tied to the bindings already secured on the bed frame—which happened to be at the window, thank God—she stripped off the bed's sheets and tied them together as well. She needed some way to get fully down the three stories, and she didn't have many options.

She wished she could cut or rip the sheets into strips, but she had no real time to do that and didn't want to make the noise either. One of the sheets was ripped though, and she studied it for a moment and then quietly ripped it all the way down, then tied the pieces together and threw her makeshift rope outside. That would at least get her down one more floor.

The more she did, the more she panicked she became that her kidnapper and the damn buyer would return before she was done.

If she had to fall twenty feet, it might break an ankle, and she couldn't do a lot about that, but she'd do what she could. Besides, she only had so many options and wouldn't lie here and be some bloody guy's *gift*. Or purchase. That was the worst thing, just knowing that this was happening to her soon, and she could do only so much to stop it. But she'd do her damnedest.

And, with that, and nothing useable left except for the mattress, she looked at it and smiled. Then she grabbed it and threw it out the window, knowing that that would alert anybody on watch below, but it would hopefully give her something soft to land on. As soon as it fell, she immediately heard the pounding of feet beyond her door. And so, hanging on to the sheet, she jumped out the window and climbed down.

There had to be a way to get to the bottom and a way to save her ass from all this. From the looks of her kidnapper, he could just as easily yank the sheets and her right back up and through the window with no problem. This escape plan of hers was just too stupid to even contemplate as possible, but it was what she had.

As soon as she climbed along the blanket to the sheet, she heard shouting above. She immediately slid as fast as she could, going all the way down. And, when she ran out of sheets, she dropped to the ground. Luckily she hit the mattress, but she rolled, jumped up and headed around the corner as fast as she could. For all she knew, her captor was already here on the ground, outside, waiting for her. And that would be too damn bad. She would do the best she could, and, if it was not quite enough, she'd deal with it. But she'd go down trying.

She whipped around the corner, and, as soon as she got there, she raced forward, only to slam up against a vehicle. She hit the front of the hood, rolled up the windshield and bounced off the rooftop, even as people around her screamed and yelled. And then she raced to her feet, limping and struggling as she tried to get away.

When two people came to her, one a woman, Vanessa screamed, "Help me! Help me! They kidnapped me and were keeping me prisoner up there."

And she pointed to where the sheet and blanket were being lifted up over the windowsill again. And that's the last thing she remembered, as she put her weight down on her foot, and the pain shrieked up her spine. If she hadn't broken her ankle, she had damn-near done a good job of it, hurting it one way or another. She'd be lucky if she survived one more step. But then she saw her captor on the street. She pointed him out and said, "That's him. There! He's the man who kidnapped me."

He took one look, pointing his finger at her, and said, "I'll be back," then bolted.

Vanessa tried to go after him, seeing where he went, when the pain rocketed up her leg, and she went down, smacking her head on the concrete. And that was it. Darkness took her over.

MILES'S PHONE RANG as they raced toward their interview. He answered it and said, "Yeah, what's up?"

"Disturbance at," and he was given an intersection, which Miles immediately punched into the car's GPS, and then Nico pulled the vehicle into a U-turn in the middle of the street with screeching tires all around them. The caller continued, "A woman just escaped, saying she'd been kidnapped. She's hurt, but she got herself out. An ambulance is at the scene right now, and we think it's her."

"Her?"

"Vanessa," the voice said. "You need to get there fast. A crowd has gathered, and it's chaos."

"We're on the way," Miles said. "Be there in five."

"Faster than that," Nico said.

Miles put down his phone and looked at Nico. "Well, remember what I said about how Vanessa needs to be aware and paying attention and to stand on her own two feet? It looks like she did this rescue job all on her own," he said with a proud smile.

Nico nodded and returned his smile, then called the police station, canceling their two interviews and asking for a plainclothes detective to follow both interviewees until further notice and hung up.

As they reached the scene, the ambulance pulled away.

Nico asked Miles, "Do you want to follow her to the hospital or get details from the scene?"

"I want both," he said. "Drop me off here, and you go after the ambulance." Then he quickly approached a few people and asked them for details. The gist of it was, she'd climbed out a window, dropped onto a mattress on the ground and then got hit by a car but got back up again. As she was leaving, her captor came after her. Miles didn't hear anything new or different as the cops took official statements. On that note, Miles headed toward the hospital on foot, taking another fifteen minutes to get there.

As he walked in through the front doors, he texted Nico and asked where he was.

The answer came back immediately. **Emergency.**

Miles joined him there and asked, "Any idea how badly hurt she is?"

"Not so bad that she has to stay much longer than maybe overnight, yet not so good that she can be alone," Nico said quietly. "The blow from the vehicle hit her pretty severely. She's got abrasions and bruising all along her lower abdomen. She's badly bruised her ribs but they aren't broken. And her ankle? We don't know if it's broken or just sprained at this point in time."

"From the jump out of the window?"

"It's possible. Or from the car hitting her? I don't think anybody really knows yet. She's unconscious."

"That's not good," Miles said. "Head injury?"

"They don't know. None of the bystanders could say, and, when the emergency personnel arrived on scene, Vanessa came around, but she couldn't say either. She passed out almost immediately as soon as they started working on her."

"Which means it's likely a concussion," Miles said with a nod. "Can I see her?"

"She's already in a private hospital room, probably awaiting tests or the results. They're not letting anybody in right at the moment," Nico said, pointing at her room.

Miles snorted at that and, when he stepped inside, found one nurse at Vanessa's side.

"Only family is allowed here," the nurse said.

He walked straight to Vanessa on the hospital bed and picked up her hand, then immediately held it against his cheek. "And fiancés," he whispered. God, he hated to see the flaxen look to her skin. Her expression was not a calm stillness but instead an almost stirred sense of being in a panic mode underneath. He cupped her cheek and whispered, "It's okay now. You'll be just fine." He leaned over and kissed her gently, brushing the hair off her freckles, knowing this was real, not some act.

Then he turned to the nurse, glared and barked, "How bad is it?"

She smiled at him. "Not so bad. She'll survive. She took quite a blow."

"She's incredibly resilient," he said, squeezing Vanessa's fingers lightly. He glanced at her ankle and frowned. He could see the swelling already evident. "I don't like to look of that," he muttered. The alignment was good, but it was pretty well black and blue already.

"No, but considering some of her other injuries," the nurse said, "the ankle will heal fast enough."

"Do we have X-rays back yet?"

"No, not yet," she said. "We just got her back from X-ray though, so at least she can rest undisturbed for now. We're waiting on the results."

He pulled up a chair and sat, then dropped his forehead to her arm and held his position while the nurse left. At that point, he lifted his head and stared at the beautiful woman on the bed, then whispered, "That was an incredibly brave and very risky thing you just did. And I'm so grateful you did it." He knew she would be as well, if and when she ever woke up, but, at the moment, she was struggling. She was unconscious and showing no signs of coming back. Or, at least, he didn't think so.

But then she opened her eyes, looked at him and asked, "Who the hell are you?"

He grinned at her and whispered, "For now I'm your fiancé."

She shook her head, her eyes diamond hard. "I don't have one," she said. "And I've had enough of strange men determining who and what I am in life to them."

He nodded and whispered, "Special Ops. Came here to rescue you, only to find out you had rescued yourself."

Hearing that, her demeanor changed a bit. That or it could be the meds she was on too.

"No," she said, struggling, her eyes closing on her. "He said he'd come after me. I'm not out of danger." She gripped his hand hard. "Please don't let him get me again."

Then her eyes closed, and she was out cold once more.

CHAPTER 4

VANESSA SEEMED TO surface and awoke multiple times, and every time she had a terrible realization that she was still a prisoner because she was so caught up in her nightmares. When she finally woke and could get her wits about her, she glanced around, and she was in a different room entirely. Relief washed through her and almost flooded her senses to the point of tears.

Immediately a voice beside her whispered, "It's all right. You're safe now. You're in a hospital, and you'll be okay."

At the voice, she frowned, turned and looked at a man she distantly remembered. "Who are you?"

"My name is Miles," he said. "I came looking for you, only to find out you had escaped by yourself."

And, with that, the rest of the pieces fell into place. She stared at the man who'd been with her before she had crashed the last time. "What the hell happened?"

"We're not exactly sure," he admitted. "We'll find out though."

"My kidnapper said a man, a buyer, was coming to check me over to ensure I was *good enough*." She tried hard not to let the pain and fear come through her voice, but she could still hear it in her tone. She gave a small head shake and then cried out as the pain slammed up against her skull.

He placed his hand on her cheek to steady her. "It seems

you tied the sheets together and dropped out of a three-story window onto a mattress, and then you got up and ran away," he said gently, "but a car hit you. You hit the front end, rolled up onto the windshield and then collapsed on the concrete. You may have some head trauma to go along with the ankle and a few bruised ribs and some very bruised innards."

She stared at him, her mind still fitting the new pieces of information into place. What she thought she'd known fell into disarray, but then slowly the pieces were picked up and put into the right place again. "I had to get out. He finally left me alone and told me that this person was coming." Then her eyes widened. "But I saw him, the guy holding me," she said, bolting upright and then crying out in agony, her body twisting in on itself.

Miles stood and sat gently on the bed beside her. "You have to stop moving."

"Now you tell me," she gasped out in pain. "Oh, my God, the pain." Tears fell from her eyes.

A nurse came in just then. "She woke up?"

"Woke up and bolted up," he said quietly. "Now she's overcome with pain."

The nurse immediately walked over and adjusted the IV. "It'll ease back in a few minutes," she announced.

Vanessa sobbed. She wanted them all to go away—well, maybe not this guy at her bedside—but, more than that, she wanted this horrible gut-wrenching pain to go away. She wanted to go back to the day she'd been in her apartment and just forget about going to a photo shoot. It didn't matter that she'd made the arrangements for it. She never wanted to live with this new reality again.

The nurse had been correct though, and, after a few

more moments, as the pain meds finally rolled through her bloodstream, she relaxed and quietly recovered from that excruciating pain. As she laid here, she heard the man whispering, "Just breathe. Take a long moment and just breathe. You'll be fine. You're safe. And I understand that he said he would come after you. And, when you're feeling better, we'll work on identifying who this man is."

She gave an almost imperceptible nod and said, "Okay. But not right now. Maybe not even today."

"It needs to be today," he said, his voice firm. "The longer we postpone it, the easier it is for him to hide."

"He's done this before," she said. "Many times."

"All the more reason," Miles said, "to make sure we stop him now. You don't want to be looking over your shoulder every day of the rest of your life."

No, she certainly didn't. And that sounded like an absolute nightmare. A life sentence of fear. "And what about the man who was coming to check me over?"

"I'm sure that meeting has been called off," he said. "But we do have men stationed outside the building where you escaped, while others are already inside and doing a search."

"Hopefully they know which room I was locked up in," she said.

"The last word I had was the entire apartment had been emptied. Including the bed and the sheets you used."

She shook her head. "But not the mattress," she whispered, a note of triumph in her voice. Maybe she'd beaten him after all.

He smiled down at her. "No, that's been taken to forensics. If we can find other people's DNA on it, that would be good."

"But there were sheets and a blanket," she muttered.

"So …"

"Even though the sheets and the blanket are gone, the mattress will still be tested thoroughly," he said. "That's not for you to worry about."

She gave a broken laugh. "I have nothing to do but worry now. That asshole got away."

"Maybe," Miles said. "But remember. You did too. That's what you need to focus on. You need to heal. We need you to get strong and to stay safe."

She gripped his fingers only now realizing she'd been holding his hand the entire time, so tight that she put half-moon crescents on the back of his hand. She stared at him and winced. "I'm so sorry."

"No, don't be. This is nothing. I'm just grateful you were enterprising enough to get yourself out of that situation."

"And then I got hit by a car," she said brokenly. "Dear God, how could I be so unlucky?"

"Don't take this the wrong way," he added, "but, by doing that, you brought a crowd of onlookers, an ambulance and police to the scene. If you had just raced off, for all you know, somebody else was tracking your movements, and they would have found you again."

She shifted ever-so-slightly so she could stare up at him. "That's guaranteed to stop me from sleeping ever again."

He nodded. "I get that, but I'm more concerned about keeping you safe."

"And capturing that asshole."

"Do you remember anything he said to you?"

"He didn't say much at all. I wasn't allowed to say anything until the gag was off."

"So start from the beginning, and tell me what you do

remember."

"I remember walking out of my apartment building, going up to the street corner to cross it—to walk a few blocks to my photo shoot," she said. "And maybe somebody pushed me or I might have felt a pinprick. I don't even know anymore. And that's all I remember, until suddenly I wake up …" As she laid here in the bed, with Miles holding her hand and making her feel more or less safe and secure, she thought about the asshole and that tone of voice. "There was something about the way he said everything," she said slowly. "As if he'd said it thousands of times over. Maybe not thousands but dozens and dozens of times."

"As in with previous prisoners?"

"Yes," she said, casting her mind back. "I think he said as much. But he was completely detached as he told me to lie there quietly, to not fight, to get up and swing my legs off the edge of the bed. I don't know if I can explain it, but he expected to be obeyed. He said I was one of the smart ones."

"I rather imagine he didn't expect you to escape."

"No," she said, puzzled. "As if I fell into one of two categories of women. Those who fought early on and those who didn't fight at all."

"Instead though, you gathered your wits about you, and, when you saw an opportunity, you took it."

"Driven by the fact that somebody was coming to inspect me," she said with emphasis. "To make sure I was 'good enough.' And I got the impression I would be stripped nude and potentially checked in more invasive ways as well." Her words were bitter. "How can somebody do that to another person?"

"Did you get the impression that it was a sexual thing or more of you being bought and sold like cattle?"

She slowly rolled her head to the side and stared up at him. "With him, definitely like cattle," she whispered, the horror still impacting her. "But I was much more worried about the sexual element from the buyer." She clenched her fingers even harder. "Dear God, if he ever gets ahold of me again …"

"Which he won't," Miles said firmly. "Any chance you can work with a sketch artist to see if we can get his face on paper?"

"I can try. I certainly saw him. At least I think I did. He wore a black hat, black sunglasses and had a beard when I saw him inside my room—but not when he was out on the street," she realized. "He pointed at me then and told me how he was coming after me."

"But how did you know it was him?"

She frowned, nodded, thinking for a bit. "He was wearing the same plaid shirt, rolled up past his forearms. He had a tattoo too," she said suddenly. "I don't know if I can remember it though, but it was almost like the wheel of a ship."

Miles sat back with an odd look on his face.

"What's that mean to you?"

"Nothing for the moment, but it's a popular maritime tattoo," he said. "Now, I want you to rest, and I'll get a sketch artist in here."

As he stood, she cried out and gripped his hand. "You can't leave me alone. He's coming for me."

"I know," Miles said. "He said he was coming for you, and we'll make sure that, if he does come, somebody else is here waiting for him."

She shook her head. "That's not good enough." He hesitated, and she stared up at him, struggling with the rising panic and with the knowledge that she needed him with her. "I want you here with me at all times," she snapped, some of her temper rising. "Otherwise I won't talk to a sketch artist."

His eyebrows shot up. "So you want another woman caught because your demands aren't met?"

Immediately she backed down because, of course, the next woman in line could potentially be her own sister. "I don't mean it that way," she said, a note of desperation in her voice. "You have to understand. I'm just terrified he'll capture me again."

"I will stay as long as I can and as often as I can," he said in a firm but gentle voice. "And I promise, if I'm not here, I'll make sure somebody who's equally concerned with keeping you safe and alive is by your side."

She had to be happy with that because, of course, for all she knew, he had a wife in labor and couldn't stay. "Fine," she said, giving in. "But please, dear God, don't leave me alone for him to find."

"I'm only going to the door," he said. "I'll speak to somebody who's standing guard outside."

As soon as she realized another guard was out there too, she relaxed even more. "And maybe if you're talking to people," she said, "is there any chance for a cup of coffee?"

He flashed a grin at her. "A woman after my own heart," he said briskly. "I'll make sure we get coffee for two."

She watched, hating to see him even walk away from the bed as he headed to the door. But, as if knowing that, he opened the door and used his foot to prop it open as he spoke to the guard on the other side. As soon as that was done, he pulled out his phone, and, although he wasn't close enough for her to hear the conversation, it appeared to be short and to the point. Then he walked back, sat down beside her and said, "There. That wasn't too painful, was it?"

She let out a deep, shaky breath and shook her head. "Thank you," she said. "I'm being foolish, I know."

"Not foolish at all," he said, his beautiful smile so warm and compassionate.

The panic inside her eased even more.

"It's totally normal for you to realize now, that you are safe, what all could have gone wrong with your escape. It's your body's way of ridding itself of those fears. Like crying helps with depression and anger. Like a fever fights the germs. It's a natural process, just one you probably haven't encountered in your life. But you'll get through this aftermath just like you got through the kidnapping event itself. It's just as important to look after your own well-being right now as anything else. We'll catch this guy. Don't you worry."

"Before he captures someone else?" Her eyes filled with tears. "Something was just so detached and automated about his movements, as if he didn't give a damn about who I was, where I came from, or my hopes, my dreams, anything," she cried out.

He leaned over and gently cupped her cheeks, then whispered, "Because he didn't. He has no humanity left. That's what you have to remember. He's mentally sick, full of evil. But you can't focus on how he sees things. After all, you're just a number to him. Potentially a piece of meat to be sold. But that's not who you are. Not by a long shot. This madman has no emotions attached to what he's doing, except maybe now anger. Because, if he's done this before, and yet you've escaped, you could be the only one who successfully evaded him. Remember that."

"And I think that's why he left me alone. In his mind, I

fit into a certain category of woman, and he'd seen it time and time again, and I could do nothing to surprise him. So he was fine to leave me alone. As soon as he did …" She shook her head. "I did everything I could to get out."

"And what you did was amazing," he said. "It saved your ass."

And, with that, she gave a shaky laugh and nodded. "Thank you for that. Although I have to admit, my ass is feeling pretty damn sore right now."

"Well, you didn't have quite-enough padding to stop that vehicle," he said, "so your body's taken a heck of a blow. Do you need to shift your position at all?"

"I'm not sure," she said. "I was hoping I didn't have to get out of bed to make it to the bathroom, but I guess I'll have to, won't I?"

"I don't know if you have a catheter or not," he said. "Let me find you a nurse."

He got up and walked to the door, but she called out, "Miles?" At the doorway, he turned. She whispered, "Can you make sure you stay inside?"

He gave her a reassuring smile and nodded. "I was just sending the guard to get a nurse for us."

She sagged onto the bed and whispered, "Thank you."

She'd always had nightmares about being attacked after one of her father's friends had come into her bedroom when she was only six. That had set her up for a lifetime of nightmares. She'd slept with the lights on for a decade, at least. And now? She knew she'd probably never sleep in the dark again—if she slept at all. But Miles stayed with her, true to his word. And she realized that maybe, just maybe, she would get through this nightmare after all.

BY THE TIME Miles brought a nurse in to assist Vanessa to the bathroom, the coffee had arrived. He helped set it up, so she could get back into the hospital bed with her coffee at her side. He didn't know if she would need food or not. He sat back down and quickly sent out messages on his phone, giving both Nico and Ryker updates. Then he got a message saying that the sketch artist would be here in twenty.

As far as he was concerned, it wouldn't be fast enough. But she might need a little more bolstering than just a cup of coffee. He frowned, wondering if she'd had much food or when. He went back out to the security guard and asked, "Can you round her up some food? We've got a sketch artist coming, but she might need a bit of sustenance to get through the process."

Understanding crossed the guard's face, and he said, "I can have somebody bring up something for her."

"Good idea," he said, and he returned to the bed in time to see her coming out of the bathroom.

When she saw the coffee, her face lit up.

"I've got some food coming for you too," he said. "Plus the sketch artist will be here in twenty."

She nodded slowly and, with the nurse's help, crawled back under the covers. But she was pale and sweating by that time, and she collapsed again. She wouldn't be moving anywhere today at all. As soon as the nurse was ready to leave, he stopped her at the doorway and asked, "Any idea how long she'll stay?"

The nurse shook her head. "At least tonight. But it could be longer than that. We're concerned about the soft tissue damage."

He nodded and headed back over. "You managed to hobble on your ankle, so that's good."

She gave him the briefest of smiles. "Don't know about that," she said. "But at least I got to and from the bathroom, so that part is good, yes."

As soon as she was settled, he got up and moved the little table, then swiveled it closer to her so that she could reach her coffee. She picked up the cup and smiled, took her first sip. "This tastes so good," she whispered. She blew on the top and took a second sip and then took a bigger sip. She waited a few moments, had a fourth sip and then relaxed back. "I'm still struggling to believe it's over," she whispered.

He smiled at her. "It'll take time. And it could be a lot of time. It could, in theory, be something like a year or two. But you take all the time you need to deal with this."

She rolled her head toward him, wincing only a little bit this time, and whispered, "I was attacked when I was six. I never slept with the lights off for at least ten years."

He leaned forward. "Can you tell me about that?"

"Nothing to tell," she said. "One of my father's friends decided he wanted a little girl in his bed. He was drunk, and he came to rape me. My little sister woke my father up because I was screaming and being held down, but, because of the noise, she ran to get Daddy. As it was, nobody pressed charges, but the guy was consumed by guilt and ended up drinking himself to the point where he walked in front of a car about six years later and died. But he should have been charged. He should have gone to jail, and nobody gave a shit about that at the time."

"Why is that?" he asked in outrage.

"Partly because my father was in a business that didn't need the negative publicity and partly because I was so traumatized I wouldn't talk to anybody about it," she whispered. She gave Miles a half smile. "So I already know what recovery is like. This more recent event, in a way, was way worse," she said, "because of the potential for a more horrific outcome there. Back then, yes, I likely would have been raped and possibly killed, but I think the drunk guy was more about getting his own rocks off than anything else at the time. Although I would have been further traumatized, I would have potentially lived and had a future of my own making. This situation today was not about me having my own future at all. This was about me being in prison for the rest of my life and potentially bought and sold many times over. It's not anything I want to even consider, much less remember."

"Yet," he said, "the best thing we can do is bring it to a conclusion. You've got to speak up. There's some magic involved in that old axiom about *confession is good for the soul.* Part of the reason you had nightmares back then is because you never got resolution from the earlier attack."

"Maybe. But I was pretty young. I ended up seeing a therapist when I hit puberty. And then I grew up and had relationships with men," she said with a mocking smile. "I found I couldn't tolerate even the slightest weight of somebody on top of me."

He nodded in understanding. "And I think that's a fairly normal reaction from an adult who'd been traumatized like that when a child. You're lucky your little sister saved you back then."

"And she's probably going absolutely nuts right now," Vanessa whispered. "Does she know I'm safe?"

"I'm not sure," he said. "Do you want to call her?"

Her eyes opened up wide, and she nodded. "May I?"

He held up his phone and asked, "What's her number?"

She rattled it off, and he quickly punched it in. When a woman answered in an exhausted and a fearful voice, he said, "I'm a special investigator. My name's Miles. Somebody here wants to speak to you." And he handed his cell over to Vanessa.

She whispered, "Ruby?" And then the two women started to bawl.

He stepped away, going to the door and pushing it open, so he could look out in the hallway, but he kept a partial ear on Vanessa's phone call. The security guard looked at him with a raised eyebrow, and Miles nodded toward the inside.

The guard swiveled enough that he could look in at the woman crying in the bed on the phone, and he nodded. "At least she's alive to tell about it," he murmured.

Miles couldn't agree more. He was still waiting for her food and for the sketch artist but hoped that she had at least ten minutes to take this time with her sister. "It would be good if we could have the food first and then the sketch artist." But he knew that things didn't always work out in his preferred time frame. A trolley was wheeled toward him. He studied the orderly and stiffened. "I've got no reason to suspect him, but …" he said to the guard.

"I do," the guard said. "I haven't seen him before."

Miles nodded. "As far as I'm concerned, anybody here right now is suspect. She's been openly threatened that he'll come back after her."

The orderly stood straight and smiled at them. "Food was requested," he said. "I'm from the kitchen." His name tag and face and photo ID all matched, but the guard still took a step off to the side and made a phone call, while Miles lifted the lids on the various platters and checked them further.

"Good, thanks," Miles said. "I'll take it inside." And he pushed the trolley into the room, still blocking the doorway with his body.

"Hey, I'm just doing my job," the orderly said with a big smile.

Miles smiled and said, "Then you won't mind if we take your picture, will you?"

The man stared at him in shock and raised his hands and said, "No, I don't mind. I guess this is a big deal, huh?"

Miles quickly snapped a photo of his features and said, "Let's just say, nobody'll be assumed to be a good person here."

The guy nodded and smiled. "It's a shitty world when people hurt others," he said. "I need the trolley back whenever you're done. Just leave it out here, and I'll collect it later."

"Will do," Miles said. He turned to the guard and said, "Did you check him out?"

The guard nodded. "Been here ten years."

"Says he works in the kitchen," Miles said.

"Yeah, the call confirmed that."

"Guess that's why we haven't seen him around then, isn't it?" Miles said, and he walked back into her room, shutting the door again. She was still sniffling, but his cell phone was in her lap. He walked to the bathroom and picked up a spare roll of toilet tissue and brought it to her. "It's not pretty Kleenex," he said, "but it might help."

She smiled a watery smile but still held a bright sense of joy in her expression and said, "I didn't ask, but my sister is coming down regardless."

"That's fine," he said with a smile. "As long as we can

clear security to let her in."

"My sister would never hurt me," she whispered.

"Good," he said. "That makes you the better kind of siblings."

She nodded. "She's always looked out for me. It's a complete reversal. I should be looking out for her, my baby sister. But, after what happened to me as a child, it was an automatic role that she took on."

"Good," he said. Then he pushed the trolley beside her. "How about some food?"

"I'm not sure I can eat," she said.

"I know," he said, "but the sketch artist will be here in the next ten minutes or so, and I thought maybe something in your stomach, outside of the drugs and the coffee, might help calm your nerves."

They adjusted her bed, so she could sit up a little bit more, and then he brought over several of the dishes for her to take a look at. A beef pie was in one, and she smiled and said, "That's so very British. I'll have that." And he gave her a fork, and she got about half of it down. And then she put the fork to the side and said, "I don't want to overeat. I was so damn hungry when I was kidnapped, and he did feed me, but I don't know how long ago that was. And I really want to eat more." She stared at the food. "But I don't want to get sick."

"No reason not to take it slow," he said. He motioned at the other tray. "A sandwich is in here, and a salad."

He lifted the lid and brought the plate over. She looked at it and froze at the memory. She forced herself to move past it—that nightmare was over. She was free now. Taking a deep breath, she smiled. "I'll have some salad." He quickly switched out the plates, and she ate most of the salad before putting her fork down again and saying, "That's all I can handle."

He nodded and asked, "Do you want any of this for later?"

She said, "Yes, please leave it, and I'll see if I can eat it in a little bit."

When a knock came on her door, he moved the trolley off to the side. He caught her sucking in a breath, and he looked at her reassuringly and said, "It's fine."

She gave an irritable shrug. "It might be fine for you," she said, "but I'm a long way away from feeling like everything's fine."

He smiled, nodded. "That's good. That's to be expected. Healthy even. We've got our sketch artist here, I hope."

He opened the door to see the sketch artist standing there, his ID being photographed and checked over by the guard. Miles did the same himself, taking a photograph of the man before letting him in the room.

"Well," the artist said, "I mean, I get the security, but …"

"We're not taking any chances," Miles said. He brought over a chair and had him sit down beside Vanessa. And then he introduced the two of them.

Vanessa looked at him, smiled and said, "Thank you for coming."

"No problem. Now let's get started."

CHAPTER 5

IT WAS EXTREMELY daunting to forcibly recall the man who Vanessa had met in that room where she had been held and then to see him again on the street with her. "I don't know which face I'm supposed to tell you about," she confessed. "The man I saw clearly inside the room wore a hat with sunglasses and had a beard," she said. "And I did see him several times up close and personal. The man who threatened me in the street was the same man, but he didn't have the hat or the sunglasses on at that point in time. Neither, I think, did he have a beard."

"Good. Let's start with the man you saw inside."

And, with that, she gave him the answers to all the questions he asked: the shape of her kidnapper's face, length of the beard, type of hat, type of sunglasses, and it was exhausting capturing those details from her memory. But she was reasonably pleased that she could answer everything the artist asked about. And when he showed her the picture, her breath caught in the back of her throat, and she instinctively cowered in her bed.

Miles immediately grabbed her hand. "I'll take that as a good sign that you recognize this person."

She took several slow calming breaths and then nodded. "That's damn freaky," she whispered. She nodded at the artist and said, "You're very talented."

He gave her a gentle smile. "The work I do is very diffi-cult sometimes," he admitted. "But, when we hit it right, then it's pretty miraculous. Now we'll take this image and make a few changes. And then we'll work on that next version of him." And he took the first image and handed it off to Miles, who took a picture of it. Then the artist redrew the same face but left the beard and sunglasses off. And he said, "When you saw him on the street, do you remember anything about his hair?"

"Brush cut," she said immediately, "like a military hair-cut." He nodded and drew away. She glanced at Miles, wondering at the stillness inside him. "Did I say something wrong?" she murmured. "You look angry all of a sudden."

He smiled at her. "Of course I'm angry. Any asshole who did this and thought that he should be allowed to do it again and again is not somebody who should be breathing our air."

Something else was in his tone, but she wasn't sure just what it was. She smiled and nodded. "Hopefully these drawings will help. Do you share these with all the local police stations? What happens?"

"Both of these images will be circulated around. More than that, we can start nailing down neighbors and running this through several databases to see if this person comes up with a facial recognition match."

"I guess that's why the sketch artist is so important, isn't he?" she said. "I didn't really think about that."

Miles smiled and squeezed her fingers gently again as the sketch artist asked a few more questions.

"Were you close enough out on the street to see his eyes?"

"Only to know that they had a laser vision and were locked on me, and he was furious," she said. "His jaw was really square too, by the way."

"Interesting," he murmured as he kept on sketching. And when he stopped and settled back, he asked, "What about that?" And he turned and held up the sketchbook.

She cried out and then whispered, "Oh, my God. That's him. That really is him."

The artist looked over at Miles and said, "Looks like we might have gotten lucky on this one."

"Good," he said. "I need digital copies of each for myself. Can you email that to me?"

The artist opened up his laptop with a special scanner, where he quickly scanned in both images and sent them to Miles.

"Now you need to send it out to the law enforcement agencies," Miles said. "They will all want a copy of these as well."

MILES FORWARDED BOTH sketches to Ryker and to Nico. Of Nico though, there was no sign. Miles frowned; losing track of his partner was never a good thing. He sent Nico a message. **Where are you?**

At the apartment where she was kept as a prisoner. Find anything?

Forensics is busy, he said. **I'm calling you now.**

When Miles answered, he said, "What's up?"

"Forensics is here. Her room was readily found. It's an apartment, leased by a corporation, and the contact person for the corporation says they haven't used it in a long time and were looking at putting it on the market. It was on the market several years ago, and, although they had several interested buyers, the proposed sale fell through. They leased it for a couple years to several people, and then those contracts ended, and they haven't done anything with it since."

"So it's not been used for how long?"

"Upward of three years, it's been empty."

He shook his head. "That's foolish."

"Property prices have been rising, so they were more or less waiting for the sweet spot to sell it."

"And they couldn't get anybody else to lease it?"

"They did have somebody ask, but they didn't like his references enough to sign a lease, so they refused to."

"See if you can find out who that was," he said. "And what's forensics finding now?"

Nico took a deep breath and said, "DNA. Various DNA. We're not sure how many different DNA samples were found and whether we're talking male or female yet, but it'll take time."

"So, several people were in that apartment, but can we determine how long that DNA has been there?"

"According to the company who owns the place, the rooms and carpets were all steam cleaned after the last leaseholder left, all to prepare to lease it again."

"Interesting. So we have a three-year window here."

"Yes, but it'll take days or weeks, if not months, to get all the DNA samples run and then to attempt to match them all."

Miles snorted at that. "I don't think so," he said. "We'll ask the Mavericks to kick that one up to the top. No way we'll get timely information on the serial kidnapper if we have to wait for that."

"I knew you would say that," Nico said with a chuckle.

"I've already pulled some strings, and we're hoping to get this analyzed way faster."

"It needs to be faster than way faster," Miles said. "Otherwise, how will you explain to the families that their daughters became just a number?"

"Unfortunately," Nico said, "it happens all too often."

"It's not acceptable. We have things that need to be dealt with, and, in order to do that, we need information. And, if there's forensic information, that's even more important to have."

"I hear you. I'll let you know more on that as we hear back from the labs."

"Outside of DNA, is there anything else?"

"No. Well, there's still the bed frame. The mattress went out the window, and the kidnappers took the bedding hanging out the window with them, and they left behind a little bit of furniture, but there's nothing in it."

"So potentially something could be there but maybe not. Let me know what you find."

"Will do." Nico hung up.

Miles escorted the sketch artist, who had everything packed up by now, out the door and then spoke briefly with the security guard, letting him know that, outside of the trolley meant to be picked up, nobody else should be coming by for a while except for Vanessa's sister. "And you let me know when she gets here. We want to make sure that she is who she says she is."

The security guard nodded. "Nobody's getting past me who isn't exactly who they say," he vowed.

Miles headed back inside and checked over the food scenario, then asked Vanessa, "Want anything else from the trolley?"

"I could eat right now." She studied the rest of the food on the plates and said, "Hand me the remaining meat pie." She scooped out the filling and had some of it and a couple bites of the pastry, and then she was done.

He took the entire trolley with all the dishes and put it outside. "More coffee will be good though," he said to the guard.

"I'll order some more for you." The guard nodded. "Could use one myself."

"When are you off?"

"In two hours," he said. "I'll be fine until then with just coffee."

At that point, Miles pushed the trolley out of the way against the wall between two hospital rooms and stepped back inside. The hospital seemed to be getting busier, and the sounds filtering into her room were almost overwhelming.

She stared up at him. "I wasn't expecting it to be that loud out there."

He shrugged. "Big city and big hospital. Busy place."

She nodded. "I don't spend much time in the hospital," she said. "It's not my favorite place to be."

"It's nobody's favorite place to be," he said with a smile. "I've ordered more coffee. Other than that, are you ready for a nap?"

She laid here for a moment. "I don't know if I'm ready to sleep," she said honestly. "There's an awful lot to be said for just resting here. This was pretty traumatizing."

"I'm sorry about that, that you even had to experience this," he said.

She shrugged. "At least something good came out of it."

"Absolutely," he said. "We have a face now. And you're

feeling pretty solid about that face?"

She nodded. "It's damn freaky."

"Well, we have people running it through various data-bases right now."

"I just hope we find him," she whispered. "And I really want to find the guy who was supposed to come and check me over."

"Depending on who it is," he said, "he could be flying in for this meet, and I'm sure he's been warned that the place has been compromised, so he won't be showing up."

"But he could be anywhere," she said, staring moodily out the window. "For how long will I look at every guy and wonder if it isn't him?"

"Potentially for a lifetime," he said firmly as he sat down. "But you get your nightmares under control, and you take steps to be safe out there in the world because you can't let it stop you from living a full life."

She shook her head. "It seems so bizarre. People go life-times without ever having something like this happen, and here I've been attacked twice."

"I know. It seems like some people lead lives full of charm."

"Isn't that the truth?" She laid back and closed her eyes.

"Sleep if you can," he said. He stood, and immediately her eyes flew open. He looked at her, smiled and said, "I ordered coffee, so I'm waiting for that. Afterward, I'll sit here with my laptop and do some work."

"Thank you." And shifting ever-so-slightly, she pulled the sheet up over her shoulders.

He reached over and tugged it a little more firmly and tucked it up around her. "Are you warm enough?" he asked. "There's a blanket here, if you need that too."

She nodded at the idea of a blanket, and he pulled that up over her. As soon as she was resting again, he walked to the door just in time to see coffee coming. He looked back, but she was sound asleep, so he handed one of the coffees to the guard and said, "Here. You might as well have it. She's out."

Then, with a smile, Miles stepped back inside the room and walked to his bag on the floor, pulled out his laptop and got to work.

As soon as he had it open, the Mavericks chat window opened up with a link. He clicked the link, and there was his guy. The sketches came back that fast with a ninety-nine percent match.

Military, all right, but American. Miles stared at that, feeling a wave of anger coming over him like he couldn't believe. Even worse, their kidnapper was navy. A seaman for fourteen years. John Ambrose. A forgettable name. Something that the women would smile at, nod and not even think to remember.

But then his face had that same appearance too. Brown hair. His eyes could normally be quite soft and friendly, and, if he had a smile on his face, he would probably attract a lot of women. As it was, he had a frown and an ugliness in that angry picture with the look that the sketch artist had captured. It matched the other photo they had from his service record. The photo had captured a deadness inside him.

Miles quickly scanned the seaman's record, reading *dishonorably discharged*. "Well, doesn't that just figure?" he murmured. He kept reading through to see what the problem was, and it turns out he had been a fighter, didn't get along with his coworkers and was well-known for brawling at every one of their ports. Still, Miles had seen that with a lot of guys; this anger often worked its way through their system until they were much more amiable to get along with.

But in this case, with John Ambrose, apparently it never worked. After fourteen years of this, John got kicked out, with numerous citations for bad behavior. But none of it was criminal. None of it had caused damage to the extent of anybody needing surgery or leaving the navy because of him. John hadn't killed anybody. At least none that they knew about.

Miles thought about that and wondered if that's not where all this started. It would be quite easy to see how John's career had gone in this direction. Obviously he still had rage issues that John had never successfully dealt with inside. What would make somebody so damn angry?

Miles studied the guy's face so that he would recognize him on the street. The one sketch with the hat and glasses and beard was also excellent, as it gave Miles a whole different look to Ambrose to consider. Without the sunglasses and without the beard, all different kinds of combinations were possible too though. But, with any luck, they'd find John.

When John's image was burned into Miles's memory, he closed his dossier and started researching his quarry, to find any history throughout the police records in various states and countries. Once a man like that left the navy and, particularly with the dishonorably discharged tag, Miles couldn't imagine that John's anger got any easier.

As a matter of fact, John would probably have lashed out and might have started killing people. The navy discharge had been about fifteen years earlier. Miles frowned at that, thinking about what kind of anger would cause him to go after redheads. Reopening the dossier, he found contact info and reached for his phone.

By the time he tracked down the person on the report, he'd left the service himself. Swearing, Miles went to the chat window and typed, **Ryker, I need specific information on this John Ambrose guy. I want to know why he was dishonorably discharged. And were there any redheads in his life at the time? We're looking for a reason why he's going after these specific women.**

On it.

Have you contacted the navy?

Yes, the person who wrote the report is no longer there. He was superintendent at the time. Can't see that in the report. Just then a name and a phone number popped up in the chat window.

Miles laughed and quickly dialed.

When a stern voice answered at the other end, Miles identified himself and said, "I'm looking into the history of John Ambrose."

The man snorted. "You mean, he's not in jail?"

"We're hoping to find him and put him in jail," Miles said quietly. "A woman just escaped after he'd kidnapped her and held her captive."

"That would be him," the man at the end of the phone said. "He was trouble from day one. Didn't want to be a team player, didn't want to follow any rules. And anytime he had a chance to break free, he would break free in a big way."

"And yet he stayed for fifteen years?"

"Yes, and, in all those fifteen years, he was a pain in the ass. We're not sure how much trouble he caused when he was on his leaves, but it seemed like he always was tossed into jail or had thrown somebody else into a hospital, yet nobody pressed official charges."

"But the problem wasn't just during his leaves, was it?"

"No, he'd brawl with anybody," he said. "And we highly suspect that he raped a woman. She did complain but, unfortunately then, for whatever reason, she withdrew her complaint, and it never went to a full court case. But he was the accused."

"Do you have her name?"

"Melinda Leon," he said. "She was a naval officer. And he was difficult around her, and then finally it seems like he lost it and attacked her."

"And what happened to her?"

"She retired from the navy, which was a hell of a damn shame because she was a fine officer. And I don't imagine you'll find her now," the man said. "But it's possible."

Miles had already typed the name into the chat box to ask Ryker to find her. "Do you have any idea what country she went to?"

"To England, I believe, but I'm not sure."

"And it all happened fairly quickly after the time that he was discharged?"

"It all was about the same time. She withdrew her accusations and left fairly soon afterward."

"Do you think he pressured her?"

"I'm sure of it," he said, "but we could never prove anything. And, without proof, unfortunately a lot of guilty parties end up going free."

"Unfortunately that's very true. If there's anything else you can tell me about him, I'd appreciate it," Miles said.

"Outside of the fact that he was a bully and that he was into fitness and weapons, it's hard to know what to say."

"What kind of trouble did he get into on leave?"

"Just the usual. Lots of women, drinks and then brawls."

"Did he have a particular type of woman that he liked?"

"Well, Melinda was a redhead, and he certainly seemed to go after her. Not sure that was so much of a type for him as I think he wasn't fussy about hair color."

"But then lots of guys aren't," Miles said, but inside he knew he was on the right track.

"True enough. And, if you've been on board, you know that leave is very much a case of letting off steam."

"Yes," Miles said and nodded, having a lot of memories himself. "Was he technology-oriented? Or was he much more of a grunt?"

"A grunt but sneaky. If he beat somebody up, and he got in trouble over it, he would find a way to get back at the other guy."

"*Nice*," Miles said. But, in the back of his head, a picture of this guy was forming. "Did he hold a grudge?"

"Forever," he said. "It was really getting to be a problem. He'd been warned several times, but we also had good reasons why we kept on him because he really excelled at what he did, and he could always be counted on. And, whenever there was an emergency, he was first up to volunteer. But he liked the action a little too much and liked the violence a little too much. So it all came to a head over our officers' accusations, and things blew up from there."

"So, he was discharged but never paid the price for his crimes," Miles said.

"No, unfortunately. If I could change one thing, that would be one of them," he said. "But I'm afraid, other than that, I don't have anything I can help you with."

Miles thought about it for a moment and then said, "If you don't mind, can I call you again, if I come up with anything else? Oh, and what about family? I don't see anything in this dossier."

"I believe his family is dead. I think he was an orphan, potentially raised in the foster care system, which might have added to his violent nature."

"Violence is one thing," Miles said, "but it's got to be controlled and contained. You can't have somebody going off half-cocked all the time."

"Easy to say," the man said, "but much harder to do. In some cases, you can't ever really control some guys. And Ambrose was one of them." And, on that note, he hung up, leaving Miles staring at the dossier in front of him.

He quickly researched John's family but came up with a dead end. He entered that into the chat box. **We need everything we can find about his childhood.**

Why?

Because he didn't exist before the age of twelve. And there's got to be a reason. I can't find anything, but you can surely get the information for me.

On it. And we found Melinda Leon. Although we don't have much. She committed suicide almost ten years ago. Possibly as a response to what happened to her.

Makes sense. Yet another victim. There are always so many that we can't even know them all in cases like this.

Hearing an odd sound, he looked over to see Vanessa murmuring and shifting in a panic, her body cringing away from some unseen evil coming toward her. He put down his laptop and walked over, then sat down on the side of the bed and gently stroked her hair and whispered, "It's okay. You're fine. You're safe. No boogeyman is here. Just relax."

It took a few minutes for his words and the tone of his

voice to penetrate the panic in her mind, but slowly she took several deep breaths, and her shoulders eased back, and she fell into a deep sleep again. He looked down at her and thought about her as a young child attacked by an older man and now attacked by another man and just wondered why some people's lives were sweet and filled with sunshine, and others appeared to be full of shit.

Of course he knew that, if he could ever come up with an answer to that, he'd have a billion-dollar solution for the world over. Because not just Vanessa had experienced pretty rough times in her life. But she'd been strong enough to get over the first one, and he knew she'd have to be strong to get past the second one too. She could do it. And, if there was anything he could do to help, then he was more than happy to step up and help.

His computer beeped, and he found a message in the chat box.

Ambrose legally adopted at age twelve. Birth parents died in a car crash with Ambrose inside the vehicle. No other blood-related kin alive. He was just one year old and lived. Was in the system until age twelve. A problem child from the beginning. His adoptive parents gave him their last name, Ambrose.

Miles nodded. *Explains the hostility and his first twelve years of life.* Just then came a knock on the door. Frowning, he walked over to see the security guard standing there with another woman. But she didn't look anything like Vanessa.

He frowned and asked, "And who are you?"

"Her photographer," the woman snapped. "I need to know that she's okay."

"Well, you don't get to know anything," he said in a hard voice. "You can request all kinds of things, but that doesn't mean you'll get it."

She glared at him. "I need to know she's okay. Vanessa! Vanessa!"

Immediately he stepped into the hallway, shutting the door behind him and said, "She's asleep. And you need to stop causing a disturbance. This is a hospital."

"I'm not trying to disturb her," she cried out. "We've all been so worried."

"She'll be fine," he said. "She has a couple badly bruised ribs and some bruising around her midsection, and one ankle is hurt. Other than that, it will heal."

"Her face?"

He frowned, crossed his arms, not liking what the woman asked. "If you're asking if she can still model, the answer is yes," he snapped.

The woman huffed at him. "You don't have to get upset. We're in a business, you know."

"Well, she's in the business of recovering from almost being killed," he muttered. "So take your business somewhere else. And," he said as she took several steps away, "if I hear or see any of this in the press, I'll know exactly where it came from. And you can bet I'll be on your doorstep tonight." She whirled around and glared at him. He shook his head. "Not one word."

She took two steps toward him but something in his posture or maybe the look on his face had her stopping and reconsidering her actions. Finally she gave a stiff nod and said, "Fine. But we can't keep this quiet for long."

"There's nothing to keep quiet," he said. "She's recovering in a hospital. She'll be back to work soon."

At that, she raised her eyebrows. "What does *soon* mean?"

"*Soon* means whatever Vanessa decides is soon."

"Wow, aren't you a guardian watchdog," she snapped.

"Yeah, you better believe it," he said coolly. "And you can make that a junkyard watchdog if you want. Nobody gets in or out of here without my permission."

She raised both hands in frustration. "Fine. But she has friends and family too, you know. Everybody is worried about her."

"Good," he said. He was stone-cold and detached as he studied her. "As long as everybody actually cares about Vanessa and not about themselves or some business venture, that's fine."

She shot him a look, then turned and strode away.

The security guard beside him chuckled. "She isn't a fan of yours at all."

"Don't give a shit," Miles said cheerfully. "The only ones allowed in this room are Vanessa's family. And only after we've checked and double-checked their IDs."

With that, he turned and walked back inside.

CHAPTER 6

W HEN SHE WOKE again, Miles still sat right beside her. But this time, he was buried in his laptop. She smiled, feeling reassured at his presence. She didn't know if she'd ever feel the same with any male. That didn't bode well for her life going forward if that had just become a prerequisite for her to get any rest. Or maybe there was just something about Miles.

That accent of his was beyond cute. But then she was surrounded by accents. She was in England, after all, and she was American. Well, not quite. She was born in England, but the bulk of her modeling life brought her back and forth across the pond. She was happy to be here, completely surrounded by everything she knew and understood.

Until this happened.

She'd made peace with her life up until now, and she didn't know if she was strong enough to make peace with it all over again. She wondered if Miles was correct when he said that her initial struggle had been because there'd never been any closure until this asshole from her childhood world had died. But he'd never paid for what he'd done to her, or maybe some people would say what he'd done to himself was even worse. She didn't know. She couldn't even get her mind wrapped around it.

She had talked to a psychologist several times, trying to

find peace with her world, and knew that she would have to talk to her again. Some things one didn't have to do alone, and she knew Miles would instinctively say that, right now, being alone was her decision to make. Yet she'd been the one who had insisted on him staying. He had capitulated easily enough. But still, she'd been the one almost begging him to stay at her side, and she wasn't ashamed of that at all. She shifted on the bed and groaned slightly.

Immediately he was beside her.

"I'm fine," she said. "But moving? … Well, that's not so easy anymore."

"Do you need to go to the bathroom?"

She considered it for a moment and said, "Yeah, I do. That doesn't sound like fun either."

"Do you want me to get the nurse?"

She shook her head. "I'd like to be a big girl and make it there on my own."

"Well, how about I give you a hand walking over there?" he asked. "That way we can take the bulk of the weight off the ankle, and then you can go in on your own?"

"That works," she said. She reached up a hand. "Give me your arm."

Immediately he held out his ripped and muscled arm at the ready. She placed her hand on his forearm and was amazed at how solid his muscles were. Using his arm, she pulled herself up, keeping her ribs and belly stiff, so she could swing her legs over and automatically sit at the edge of the bed. And then, with a slow and careful breath, she put weight on her feet and straightened. "It's not as bad as I thought it was," she said with a smile.

Of course that smile had dropped away by the time she made it to the bathroom. She went inside on her own, using the counter to hold her up, and then inside she took one look at her face and moaned.

Outside, she heard him anxiously ask, "Are you okay?"

"I'm fine," she said. "I just looked at my face."

"Yeah. Apparently your face is a hot commodity."

She used the facilities and then, with great effort, straightened again, shuddering as her ribs shifted with the movement. She quickly washed her hands and opened the door, so that he could see her and not panic at her moans. Then she relaxed against the wall as she asked, "Is there a towel or a washcloth?"

HE LOOKED AROUND the bathroom behind her and asked, "Isn't one in there?" He pushed the bathroom door open and stepped past her, then plucked a washcloth sitting on a side shelf at the far end of the bathroom. He held it out to her, but she hesitated. Miles watched as she judged the distance from where she stood to the sink, so he gently led her to the commode, had her sit there, while he turned on the hot water until it was as hot as he could get it, and then wet the cloth, rung it out and said, "Here. Wipe this on your face."

But when she didn't make a move—her ribs were probably still killing her—he held her head like a child, with one hand keeping her steady. Then he wiped her face to the hairline, lightly scrubbing her cheeks and her chin and her neck. "I know you want a full shower," he said. "And there's nothing worse than being held captive to make you feel dirty. Even worse to know was that this other guy was coming to check you over, but I don't think you're quite ready for a shower yet." He rinsed the cloth a couple times and then repeated his actions and wiped down her arms and hands.

She smiled at him. "It's almost like you have some experience doing this."

"No experience in doing it for other people," he said, "But I've been in lots of situations where there was no time and no place to have a shower, but a creek was close by. And it can make all the difference in the world."

She nodded.

He hesitated and asked, "Look. Your hospital gown is open in the back. Do you want me to wipe down your back? Or would you prefer that a female nurse did it?"

She nodded. "Do you mind calling the nurse?" She paused, then added, "And, while this might be awkward—for you and for me—would you stay here, at the doorway maybe, while the nurse is with me?"

"Sure. No problem."

One came quickly, and Miles carefully watched as Vanessa twisted ever-so-slightly, leaning forward on the counter now, while the nurse took a warm washcloth and gently wiped down her entire back.

She moaned. "God," she said. "That heat feels so good."

Miles nodded, adding, "And your body has taken a beating. You were skinny before, but I hope you didn't lose much weight while imprisoned. You don't have any to spare."

"I've always been slim," she murmured. "As a child, I was super thin. After the childhood attack, it was hard to get any food to stay down. And then, as a teen, it just seemed to be my natural body weight, and I never had much of an appetite."

"Want me to rinse off your legs?" the nurse added.

SHE HESITATED AND then shrugged. "Why not?" And she quickly and efficiently rinsed, washed and repeated.

By the time that was done, the bathroom door was closed, so the nurse could attend to washing her belly and chest and underarms. Vanessa would love to have a full shower, but, like Miles had said, it wasn't possible yet.

The nurse opened the door and stepped out. "Well, that's as good as it'll get for now," she said.

He nodded and stepped up to the bathroom door to assist Vanessa.

She slowly stepped out. "Another reason to hate the hospital is the lack of privacy, how everybody sees every inch of you."

"Well, I haven't seen every inch of you."

She wondered if he wanted to but banished that thought as she looked for his arm, and it was there immediately. Using it to help take the weight off her ankle, she slowly made her way forward. "I gather there's no cast, so the ankle is not broken?"

"No, it's just a sprain," he said. "I think when you landed, after the car hit you, that you probably came down on that foot at an odd angle and damaged it that way."

"If it wasn't for that damn car," she said with a shattered laugh.

"There's always something in life that comes out of left field and smacks you when you didn't see it coming," he said, grinning at her. Then, when they were at the bed, he flipped back the covers, shook out the sheets, holding them up for her, and asked, "Do you want to go back under the covers?"

"Yes," she whispered, hating a sense of shaky weakness already taking over. He helped her in bed, even swinging her legs up and around for her, and then pulled the blankets up to her chest. He'd barely gotten her settled when another knock was heard. She raised her eyebrows. "My life is even busier here than it ever was at home. Speaking of home, by the way, did anybody find my phone?"

He shook his head. "I haven't heard of them finding very much of anything at the apartment where you were being kept, so I suspect the kidnapper disposed of it."

"It has GPS," she murmured. "If somebody can check whether it's been tossed in the garbage or something, it would help."

"Actually," he said, "I should have thought of that earlier. It would give us a timeline and potentially a location."

HE WALKED TO the door first to find another redhead, younger, but much more serious-looking, standing there and hopping from foot to foot, arguing with the guard. As soon as Miles opened the door, she turned her full barrage of questions on him and peppered him continuously. The half-laugh behind him had him turning to look at Vanessa. She smiled and said, "Ruby, I'm here."

And a whole line of guards couldn't have kept Ruby contained as she dashed under Miles's arms and snuck between him and the wall to dart toward her sister. He just rolled his eyes at the security guard, who grinned like a fiend, and shut the door. He headed back to her bedside and waited for Vanessa to introduce them. He already knew who the visitor was, but …

When Vanessa could finally get a word out, she said in a rush, "Ruby, this is Miles. He's been looking after me."

Ruby looked at him, her eyes still serious and her brows pulled together into a point on her forehead as she gave him an up-down look. "A security guard?"

At that, he raised an eyebrow and crossed his arms over his chest.

"I think you just insulted him," Vanessa said. "He was tracking me down when I escaped."

"A detective then?"

Miles sighed and said, "My name's Miles, and I'll sit over here and work while you two talk. Nobody else gets in though. Remember that. So don't go inviting anybody."

Ruby leaned forward and whispered loudly, "Is he always that demanding?"

"So far, yes," Vanessa said. And the two fell into a discussion about Vanessa's injuries and what had happened. There were lots of moans and groans and cries and shock and tears as the two women shared stories of the horrors from each side. He sat down and started a text with Nico regarding tracking Vanessa's cell phone.

We can only do that when it's on, can't we? wrote Nico.

Not sure.

Right. A couple social media apps can do that. Let me take a look.

Nico disappeared off the phone for a few minutes while Miles typed in the chat box. He asked Ryker for a link as well. Instantly there was one.

It's new technology, Ryker told him. **In this case, the phone doesn't need to be on.**

Miles typed in her name and then called to her. "What's

your cell phone number?"

She gave it to him, and immediately he typed it in. She explained to her sister that they were trying to locate her phone.

"I've been calling it steadily," Ruby complained. He only half-listened to the conversation until Ruby said, "Somebody answered it at one point in time, and I was sure it was you, and I was screaming at you to answer me. But then a man chuckled and hung up fast."

Miles glanced at her and asked, "When was that?"

She stared at him in surprise and then shrugged. "Last night. Sometime around …" She pulled her phone out and checked her call history. "Ten-thirty last night."

"And somebody answered it?"

She nodded slowly. He brought out the sketches that the police artist had left them and held one of them up, then asked, "Do you recognize this man?"

She shook her head. "But, with those glasses and hat, nobody'll recognize him."

He nodded and held up the second sheet. "How about this one?"

She looked at it, frowned, tilted her head to the side and then shrugged. "It's not very distinctive," she said. "Honestly it could be a half-dozen guys."

"The jaw is very distinctive," he said. "Square."

She looked at it again. "He looks really angry." She turned to her sister. "Is this the man who kidnapped you?"

"It's the man who imprisoned me," Vanessa corrected, making a very fine distinction but also an important one. "I don't know if he's the one who initially kidnapped me."

"And you had just left your apartment and headed to the corner, and that's the last thing you remember?" asked Miles.

Vanessa reached up, checked her shoulder and said, "I think he jabbed me with a needle, some drug, and then the next thing I knew, I was being swept up and put into a vehicle. At least, I assume so. Maybe he just moved me into an apartment right beside us."

"That's a scary thought," Ruby said.

"Maybe, but it's definitely an option," Vanessa said, almost unknowingly.

He stared at her in surprise. "Interesting. You didn't mention that before."

She looked at him in surprise. "Didn't I?"

He shook his head. "Nope, you didn't."

She gave him an apologetic smile. "Sorry. It's so hard to know what I've said and what I haven't said, and, even as I talk, I get different impressions."

It was good that she was picking up bits and pieces again, but Vanessa brought up something else that made Miles wonder. He quickly tracked her apartment to the apartment where she was found, and it was literally just around the corner by two blocks. He then went back and asked in the chat box for the intel on every person from her own apartment building that he had earlier requested.

We already gathered the list of names. Two apartments are empty, and we've checked all the other residents' photos.

And no resident looks like any version of the suspect, John Ambrose?

We'll go back through the photos again, he typed. **But two of our people already went through the photos of residents in Vanessa's building, and they didn't recognize anybody there as matching the sketches.**

And there are two empty apartments?

Yes.

Who are they registered to?

One's a company, and one is somebody living in Spain right now.

Have either been rented?

Apparently not.

Considering the fact that Ambrose was using an apartment that was owned by a company, sometimes rented out, but mostly empty for three years, I wonder if these apartments are on some site, like Airbnb or whatever, and he found out about its vacant status that way and lived there without benefit of a lease.

But surely, as soon as somebody comes to check out the apartment, they would know someone was living there.

Possibly, Miles typed. **But what if Ambrose knew that these were to be listed later, but they weren't yet made public?**

Not sure how that would work, Ryker typed. **Other than through active Realtor listings.**

Right. And that would take forever, matching current rental ads to properties with no for-sale listings. Then confirming if the places were empty or if the owners were living there and had been for years. No, not an easy thing to locate these vacant-but-not-for-sale-or-rent properties, but, if there was a way to make it work, it would be a great way to find places to stay without having to worry about being disturbed and to be totally off-grid.

Other than firsthand knowledge, Ryker typed.

Right. ... Like to be that potential renter whose lease agreement was rejected. Miles snapped his fingers. *Damn. It was just that easy. Ambrose would don one of his disguises, would fill out the paperwork with one of his many aliases and waited to be rejected. Or accepted. He could want to be rejected on purpose, giving fake addresses and false references so anybody in their right mind would reject his application. Either way, he ends up with a potential place to stay. Damn.*

Ryker, get everybody you have free to contact every Realtor in all the locations where the seventeen redheads went missing and run both sketches by them, specifically asking about people wanting rentals over the last fifteen years. I doubt Ambrose used his real name, so don't mention any name right now. Just focus on a facial match. I know it's a long shot, but it's the best we have right now.

On it.

As Miles mapped out the distance between the two apartments, Miles realized just how damn close they were. A green space was between the two in the middle of the block. He looked over at Vanessa. "Did you ever spend any time on the other side of the apartments, where that green park area is?"

She frowned and shook her head. "No, not that I recall."

He looked at her sister. "What about you?"

Her eyebrows shot up. "This isn't about me."

He waited patiently for her to answer him.

She frowned at him. "I don't like the idea that you're questioning me."

"I don't care if you like it or not," he said calmly. "Any information is important to catch your sister's kidnapper—remember him?—so answer the question, please."

She glanced from Vanessa and then back at Miles and said, "I sit out there sometimes with my coffee and a sketchbook."

"On a regular basis?"

She shrugged. "Maybe. Once or twice a week? I don't know. Why?"

He ignored her sister and looked at Vanessa. "The apartment you were imprisoned in is just across that green space. Go to the end of the block, take a right at the corner, and it's the next apartment building."

She stared at him in shock. "That close?"

"Yes, so between the two buildings is the center of that square, in which there's that green space. And I'm trying to see if he would have found you there."

"But he took Vanessa from the front of the apartment building," her sister argued.

"Which would be very easy to track her back to, now wouldn't it?" And inside, he wondered if Vanessa had been the target or had Ruby been the target? Or did the kidnapper not care, as both were viable? "How old are you, Ruby?"

She stiffened and glared at him, but he wouldn't give an inch. "Answer the question, please."

"Ruby, why are you being difficult?" Vanessa asked, then answered Miles's question. "She's twenty-six."

He nodded. "And you are?" he asked Vanessa.

She groaned. "I'm twenty-eight."

He nodded and noted those down.

"You're still not explaining why you're asking me these questions," Ruby complained.

He snorted. "It wouldn't take a great leap of logic to understand that it's quite possible that you, Ruby, were chosen as a potential victim, and maybe it was a case of mistaken identity, or maybe the kidnapper didn't care, and either one of you would have worked."

The two women looked at him in horror. Vanessa cried out, "That's a terrible thing to say."

"Why? If Ruby won't answer questions that help me solve her own sister's kidnapping case just because Ruby has to know every little detail first, then I'll tell her *every little detail*," he said, his tone hard. "And then maybe she'll take a little more care when she goes home. Plus she won't hesitate to answer my damn questions."

Instead Ruby collapsed on the chair beside Vanessa. "Oh, my God," she said. "I never even considered that."

"Have you seen anybody hanging around who looked suspicious?" he asked Ruby, his gaze intent on her face.

She suddenly seemed to realize that this wasn't necessarily about her sister.

Only because she was beginning to understand and to feel some fear did Miles take it a bit easier on her. "Did that never occur to you that maybe you were targeted instead?"

She stared at him in bewilderment. "No, of course not," she said. "Why would they? We don't look that much alike."

"Yes, we do," Vanessa said. "I know you never wanted to do any modeling, but there's always been interest in you, and I've told you that before."

Ruby shrugged. "I'd rather pursue my more serious artistic pursuits."

Vanessa just rolled her eyes at that, and Miles could see it was a long-standing discussion. "What you do with your life is up to you," he said, "but you haven't answered my question. Have you noticed anybody suspicious hanging around, following you, looking at you sideways at all in the last …" He shrugged. "Let's make it a year."

She sagged even farther into the chair. "No," she said. "There hasn't been. What do you mean by a *year*?"

"Depending if this is the same guy or not," he said, "redheads have been taken at this time of year for many years."

Both women gasped and stared at him. He shrugged. "Sorry, but I think you both need to know that as well."

CHAPTER 7

"**A**RE YOU SAYING this has happened before and that the cops knew about it and that they couldn't stop it?" Vanessa asked.

"Yes," Miles said. "We've wondered just how good this kidnapper is at this."

"But ..." And words failed her for a moment. "How could they not know something about this? How could they not have caught him by now?"

"What do you mean, *them*?" Ruby asked caustically. "Why haven't *you* caught him?"

He gave her a flat stare. "Because I was only brought in on this case yesterday and just landed in London last night." That shut her up for now. He glanced over at Vanessa. "At this time of year for the last seventeen years, as far as we know, seventeen redheads have disappeared."

She swallowed hard. "Oh, my God," she said. "Is that why I was targeted? My hair?"

He nodded slowly.

She wanted to puke as the concept washed over her. She looked at Ruby to see her hand slam over her mouth as she stared in horror at Miles.

"But that's so disgusting," Ruby said. "And now, for seventeen years, this guy has gotten away with it?"

"Before you blame the police," he said, "keep in mind

that these women disappeared from different cities and different parts of this country and other countries and were different ages, not to mention were taken one year apart. However, missing women can only become a pattern when you get multiples of them going missing in the same way. And because their bodies were never found, they were always classified as missing persons, and thousands of women go missing in this country alone."

"I'm sorry, Ruby," Vanessa whispered. "I really had no idea."

"It's not your fault," Ruby said. But her tone was wrecked. "I don't know why all this keeps happening to you."

Vanessa gave a broken laugh. "Believe me. I'd be happy to have the target off my back."

Ruby nodded and jumped off her chair, then wrapped her arms around her sister and gently hugged her. "I didn't mean to make it sound like I blamed you for any of this," she said, crying. "I just wish it would all go away."

"You and me both," Vanessa said, holding her sister close.

Finally, when Ruby had calmed down enough, she looked over at Miles and said, "Any chance of getting a cup of tea and maybe something sweet, like a piece of cake or a cookie?"

Knowing the power of the chat window, he typed into the chat box, asking for just that.

She looked at him and frowned. "Aren't you going to ask the security guard?"

"I'll see what he can do as well," he said. He put his laptop off to the side and said, "For two, I presume?"

Ruby, wiping her eyes, nodded and whispered, "Yes,

please."

He looked to see it was almost teatime for them anyway. When a knock came on the door, he wasn't at all surprised. The women looked at him, both of them a little more afraid than they had been a few minutes ago. He smiled and said, "It's fine." Then he walked to the door and opened it to see Nico pushing a trolley. He let him in and closed the door securely behind him. The women stared at Nico, both with big frowns on their faces.

Vanessa looked at him and said, "I don't think I know you." Her voice was hesitant, and she did her best to bolster it up, and then she remembered. "Or maybe I do from the hospital?" She couldn't remember. She scrunched up her face and looked at him.

"Yes," he said with a smile, "from the hospital." He reached over and shook her hand. "I'm Nico, and I work with Miles."

At that, both women visibly relaxed. Ruby got up and saw the full tea service and smiled. "Now this is what we need."

Nico winked at Miles. "Apparently anything you ask for …"

Miles nodded and smiled. "I've seen it in action before."

"And did you come up with any new information?"

"A couple things," Miles said. They walked over to his laptop, and he brought up the map that he had of her apartment. "This is where Vanessa was taken from. This is where she was kept, and apparently her sister used to sit in this green space here to sketch and have tea."

Nico sucked in his breath. "Ambrose could have been watching her from up there."

"Maybe. And it's also possible that they grabbed the

wrong sister."

"And I'll never forgive myself for that," Ruby cried out.

"Hush," Vanessa said. "Much better that it was me than you."

Ruby stared at her with a wounded look. "How can you say that?"

"Because I'd do anything to keep you safe," Vanessa said with a tender smile. "You know the older sister is supposed to look after the younger one, right?"

Ruby gave her a look that said she'd heard it before. "Whatever," she said. "Age doesn't make a difference here." She looked over at Nico. "Have you found this guy yet?"

He shook his head. "Not yet but I found something else." And he pulled something from his pocket.

Immediately Vanessa cried out, "My phone."

He gave it to her and said, "It appears to still be intact. I've stripped it to make sure there's no added tracking on it, but we have to check the software too. So, although you can take a quick look at it now, you don't get to keep it for the moment."

She raised her eyebrows. Outside of turning it on and making sure her contacts were still there, she checked the number of recent phone calls and found dozens. Most of them were from her sister. She handed it back to him and said, "Maybe one of those calls is from the kidnapper. There are four unknowns in there," she said. "And generally I don't accept unknown phone calls."

"It might be," he said, "but it could be any number of people, like telemarketers, or just a misdialed number."

He handed it to Miles, who immediately connected the phone to the laptop via a cable and said, "I'll run a diagnostic and strip it. I'll move your contact list into my laptop, but everything else goes. I hope you're okay with that?"

He looked over at her, and she nodded. "I thought the phone itself was gone, so whatever. As long as I get a phone, I can put everybody back in my contacts again."

"Good," he said, and he transferred everything off the phone. He quickly ran the four numbers through a check and said, "Two of the unknown calls are from your dentist. One is from a magazine company, and the other appears to be from your insurance company."

She grinned and said, "And I really don't want to talk to any of those people."

"Give me a bit longer, and I'll scan this phone for bugs and, if there are none, I'll reload your contacts, and you can have your phone back."

"Oh, perfect," she cried out in relief.

"ARE YOU PLANNING on staying here?" Nico asked Miles, while the sisters talked among themselves.

Miles shot a sideways glance toward Vanessa and nodded, then filled in Nico about the rejected lease agreements as a way for Ambrose to find an empty rental for free and to not be on the grid. "The Mavericks team is on that, but it's beyond a long shot and covers all seventeen women's locales, and his real name probably wasn't used. So it's just a matter if someone remembers his face from the last couple decades. Realtors probably see new faces all day long. It's a long shot with horrible odds. A really massive long shot."

"Yeah," Nico agreed, "but what a great lead." He slapped Miles on the shoulder.

"We have to work any other leads as we find them and

hope something pans out and fast. Plus there is an active threat against her by her captor," he said cautiously. "I would like to go to her apartment to take a look and just to see what has been going on."

"I know," Nico said. "I've been there, and I've looked at both places, but there's nothing quite like getting that info firsthand yourself."

He stood and looked at Vanessa, then said, "I'll switch places with Nico right now."

Instantly fear whispered across her face.

Miles reached for her hand, and she eagerly reached back. "I know you're worried," he said gently. "But Nico works with me. He'll stand guard here with you, and the guard outside is still there also."

"And I'll stay for a while too," Ruby said. Both women turned to look at Miles.

Vanessa asked, "Where are you going?"

"I'll be in your home, and I'll go to the site where you were imprisoned. I need to see both places, get a good visual in my mind about what options the kidnapper was interested in and why that place was chosen and where he could have gone from there."

She hesitated.

"Yes, I can look on the satellite," he said. "And I have many times. And images are a large part of the equation, but it's not the same as getting that same feel from being in the physical location."

Her shoulders slumped, and she nodded. "No, you're right," she said. "And one day, a little bit down the road, I wouldn't mind going back through it myself. Just so I can place it in the right part of my memory, so that I have some closure there."

"When you're back on your feet, we can do that," he said.

She glanced at him, and her lips firmed up. "Any chance I can go home and rest there?"

"Not tonight," he said. "We'll talk about it tomorrow. But only if you have protection."

"Because you really don't think he knows where I live, right?"

"Are you having any doubts about that?" he asked in surprise.

She thought about it and then shook her head. "No, I still don't remember anything after going down the steps and around the corner. But, if where he held me is literally around the corner, then that makes sense that he knows exactly where I live." She grabbed her sister's hand at that. "And I don't want you going home tonight."

"I wasn't planning on it," Ruby said. "Well, that's a lie. I was planning on it. But now I'm not."

"And, by the way, you guys have a cousin who you see on occasion, right?"

The two women looked at each other and frowned. "Well, we have a couple cousins, but only one lives around here," Vanessa offered. "Yet we don't see him regularly. Why?"

Miles glanced at Nico. Both of them immediately brought up images on their phones and held them out. "He's been standing watch outside your apartment."

Vanessa looked at it, and her eyebrows shot up. "Well, that's definitely Tristan. I don't remember seeing him anytime recently. When was that taken?"

"We've tracked him twice to your place over the last year," Miles said. "So maybe they were just impromptu visits, and you were never home?"

"I saw him once," Ruby said.

"You didn't tell me," Vanessa said, rounding on her sister.

"There was no need. I saw him outside and talked to him for a few minutes, then asked if he wanted to come in. He shrugged and said, *Nah, he just found himself in the area,* and realized that we lived here. But you weren't home, and he didn't seem to want to come in if it was just me."

"I wonder what he wanted?" she asked thoughtfully.

"The same as everybody else likely," Ruby said with a smile. "Either money or connections."

"Meaning?" Nico asked.

"It's because of the business I'm in," Vanessa said. "Often people are hoping I'll introduce them to somebody in the business, or they all think that I'm making big money and can share my bounty. But, of course, it's a case of *I'll take the money and run* thing."

"Has your cousin ever asked you about that before?"

She nodded. "Once. He mentioned it in an email."

"So that falls in line with maybe what he was doing at your place?"

"It's possible."

Miles glanced at Nico and said, "I'll look him up and talk to him firsthand."

"Don't scare him though," Vanessa said.

"Do I look like I scare everybody?" Miles asked.

She nodded. "I think, if you wanted to, you'd be very good at scaring anybody."

He chuckled at that. "That sounds like a gift that I could really utilize."

"No need to scare anybody," she snapped. Some of her

feistiness was returning.

He grinned at her. "Hold that thought and definitely keep that temper. It'll help you to avoid sliding into a victim mentality."

Almost immediately her shoulders slumped. "Right. It's hard to forget that this happened."

"When you're terrified, and you're held prisoner, there's not a whole lot of ways to stay strong. Other than your mind-set. Stay strong." On that note, he slipped from the room and spoke with the guard for a few minutes, telling him where he was going and who was left inside and that nobody else was to join them. Then Miles finished with, "And I mean *nobody*."

He left the guard his phone number just in case of trouble. Then he exited the hospital and headed back to the apartments. First, he went into the apartment where she'd been imprisoned. He'd already been cleared to get in, and still police and forensics were around.

He carefully walked through, avoiding conversing with anybody, taking his own photos, studying the layout and worrying about some of it because the apartment was a little too clean—as if somebody had already had a chance to clean it or as if they didn't actually live here. What if another apartment was here where they lived but kept her in a separate one? He really liked the idea.

He pulled out his phone and quickly texted Ryker. **I need the occupants in this building where Vanessa was held. I'm looking for a second apartment that Ambrose may have used. Forensics says fingerprints were here on the walls, the little bit of furniture left behind, the bed frame, but nothing else was really left here. It was clean-clean. In other words, it's too clean, and Ambrose didn't live here.**

Ryker's response was the standard *On it,* and then Miles

pocketed his phone and went to the four neighboring apartments on this floor, knocking on doors. Three people answered. He spoke to them about the situation and quickly discarded all these occupants.

One was an older couple, avidly watching the police activity going on. Another was a single older man, smoking recreational drugs in a heavy way, the smoke filtering outside from under his door. And the third one was a middle-aged woman, who appeared to be more of a *keep to yourself* and *don't talk to strangers* type person. She couldn't help at all. She said she hadn't heard any noises coming out of any of the apartments.

Then, when nobody was watching, Miles quickly pulled out his pick and opened the door to the silent apartment across the hall from where Vanessa had been held.

As soon as he stepped in, he knew he'd been right. He closed the door silently and took photos and texted Ryker and Nico about where he was, feeling good about his choice. Ryker immediately sent a warning to be careful. And, of course, that was the trick. Just because the other apartment was empty didn't mean this one was. Miles moved through it quietly, searching to see if he was alone. He had a weapon in his side holster that he quickly unhooked and held out in front of him as he did a full sweep.

The place was empty.

He pulled out a pair of gloves that he had been offered from the forensic people and quickly put them on. If he had some proof that Ambrose may have been here, then he would get the cops over here too. But he had to have proof in order to justify a warrant. Still, this was an illegal search. Good thing he wasn't held to those standards.

However, by the time he got to the bedroom, he had more than enough proof. Pictures of Vanessa were all over the table in the sitting area here. In various positions too: tied up while lying on the bed on her back, lying on the bed on her side. Pictures were taken when she wasn't even aware of it. As he shifted them gently around on the table, he found more photos of her outside her apartment, walking the street. He quickly stepped from the apartment and crossed the hallway, then called Ryker.

"Yes," he said. "I've just sent you and Nico a bunch of photos. We need a warrant to get into this second apartment, and we need it now."

"Hold on," Ryker said. "Do you want to do a full sweep on the place first?"

"Yes, but the forensic team is here across the hall. I just don't want them to leave."

"I'll get somebody to call you."

"Fine. I'm going back in then." He headed back in and did as careful of a sweep as he could, checking drawers and cupboards and looking for anything to help confirm this asshole's identity and hopefully his current location. He took pictures every step of the way. With the bed's rumpled sheets and blankets, it was obvious somebody was currently living here. Clothing was in the closet and in the drawers, and it wasn't hard to immediately picture somebody around five foot ten or eleven inches with a size thirty-four waist and a large shirt collar.

With that physical image in mind, Miles worked his way around the bedroom, searching the night tables. Anything to give him that extra hint. When his phone rang, he quickly answered it to find somebody official on the other end, saying the warrant was coming through and to stay out of the apartment.

"Will do," he said cheerfully. He put away his phone, left the bedroom and took one last look through the living room, then stepped out into the hallway again. While waiting for the forensics crew to arrive, he went through the photos that he'd taken.

Then he texted Nico. **The asshole's been using the apartment across from where he held her. That's why forensics wasn't finding anything in the first apartment. There's nothing to find. He only went into the room where she was kept and then left.**

Nico called him just a few moments later. "Are you serious?"

"Yeah, then I found the only other apartment that was vacant in the building was just across the hallway, so … I checked it out."

"Shit," Nico said. "I didn't even think of that."

"No, because everybody was so focused on what we'd found that they didn't think about what we didn't find. And what we didn't find was any trace of Ambrose. If there's no trace of him, he wasn't there. Or at least barely was there."

"Makes sense," Nico said. "I'll pull a history on the ownership of that second apartment."

"Yeah. And find out what's the holdup on the name on that rejected lease from three years ago on the apartment where Ambrose held Vanessa. They're a damn corporation. They've got to have organized records on this shit."

"I'm on that too."

"I'm waiting for the warrant to come, and then forensics hopefully will go from that apartment to this one."

"And somebody has been living there?"

"Yeah. You'll see when the photos come through. Half a dozen pictures are of Vanessa tied up on the bed in the other apartment across the hall and some of her walking outside her own apartment in the street."

"Bastard," Nico said.

"Exactly," he said. "What we don't know is who owns

this apartment. If you can run that down right now, that would be perfect. And then get me a visual on the owner and see where this little bugger is."

"Well, I have a name, but I'm not sure it'll be of any value," Nico said with a hard sigh. "*John Smith.*"

"Wow. That's so original," Miles said. "But please tell me we have visuals on him?"

"I'm looking. It's a rental, so he should have provided some picture ID." Then, after a while, he said, "Got it. I'm sending it now."

"Is it our guy?"

"It's close enough that it could be," Nico said. "We already know this guy's got a lot of disguises."

And, sure enough, as the phone call ended, and the photo arrived, Miles could see that it was the same guy with a beard and sunglasses but no hat. "Show it to Vanessa," he said as soon as he called back again. "See if she recognizes him."

"I already did," Nico said, "and that's an affirmative."

"Okay, so we've got where the guy's been staying. At least temporarily, and we have yet another version of a facial recognition on him. Can you contact Ryker via the chat window and get him to circulate that third image around, to the local authorities but also Interpol, MI5, MI6, whatever. And don't forget the Realtors. The alias will be of absolutely no help."

"Got it. Typing up something now. If we could at least get a fingerprint from one of Ambrose's two apartments, then we might get some confirming ID."

Just then a series of officers ran up the stairs with somebody in a suit in the front. "Gotta go," he said to Nico. He looked at them with interest. The gentleman in the suit stopped and looked at him. "Are you the one who reported this?"

He crossed his arms across his chest and said, "Reported what?"

The man frowned.

Miles just raised an eyebrow.

"Are you the special operative who reported this?"

"Yes. Did you get a warrant?"

He nodded. "Yes. Anybody in there?"

He shook his head. "But I don't want everybody going in there and corrupting the scene. We need forensics over here now."

"They're coming," he said, "but I want to go in and take a look first."

"That's fine, but you're not taking everybody in here."

"They do know how to do their jobs," he snapped.

"Good," Miles said. "Then they won't even ask to go in, will they?" He kept his voice cheerful and light but his gaze was hard as stone. "We can't take any chances with this guy."

The man nodded stiffly and stepped around him, then turned the doorknob and shot him a look.

Miles shrugged and said, "Amazing. It was unlocked."

But the new arrival shook his head and stepped in. Immediately Miles followed. The detective looked at him and frowned.

"You didn't identify yourself, and I didn't see the warrant," Miles said coolly. "For all I know, you're an associate of this kidnapper."

Instantly he brought out his ID and held it up, but, instead of just flashing it at him, Miles snatched it from his hand and studied it, then took a photo of it and handed it back.

"Are you always this careful?"

"Always," Miles said.

CHAPTER 8

"HE WAS RENTING two apartments?" Vanessa asked.

"It looks like it," Nico said. "One to keep you in and one that he lived in across the hall."

"Well, maybe if he's been living there, they can find something," she said. "This is good news, right?"

"It's very good news," he said. "When we consider all that could have been missed because of this, it's very good news, indeed."

"The kidnapper's good at what he does, isn't he?" She searched Nico's devilishly attractive smiling face. There was something about Nico that was just as attractive as Miles, and yet she thought Miles was so much more handsome. Miles had a soothing natural grace and was unaware of his good looks. She wanted to distrust it, but she instinctively trusted him. Maybe because he'd been here with her and for her ever since her rescue.

She didn't even understand how she had managed her escape. And she really couldn't call it a rescue; it was an escape. She got herself out of that mess. What she had to do now was make sure she stayed out of it. "I didn't even see the apartment I was in," she muttered. "I was so focused on getting out that window."

"And that's a good thing you did," Nico said gently. His phone buzzed then. He looked down and said, "It's Miles."

He lifted it to his ear and answered it while she watched. She only heard half the conversation, but, even then, he turned, and he walked farther away and lowered his voice.

She waited, chewing on her bottom lip and wondering what was going on. Her sister had taken off to get them fancy coffees, thinking that it might be just the pick-me-up that Vanessa needed. She had to admit she was a pretty big fan of lattes and cappuccinos and various other coffee drinks. It was her one indulgence. Being a model, she couldn't do very much in the way of treats for herself, but coffee was one that she did allow. She was already starting to flag again energy-wise.

The doctor had been in earlier, almost as soon as Miles had left. After checking her over, he'd said that he wanted her to stay overnight, and then they'd see how the bruising and her other injuries were. She had only then heard about the stitches at the back of her head. They hadn't bother her when she laid down, probably because of any numbing gel and painkillers. But, since there was no concussion, it could have been much worse. She'd thought something was in her hair, but, as she had explored the area, she found a couple sutures. No wonder she had a headache.

When Nico finally came back, she studied his face and asked, "Good news or bad news?"

"Well, they found dozens of photographs of you in the second apartment," he explained gently. "So the police know they're on the right track. Forensics is working on it. They've picked up a couple fingerprints but don't know whose they are yet."

"Well, fingerprints would also be good news. Photographs at least to link him to my case," she said. "And I know that's good news, but I feel sick to my stomach." As a matter of fact, her stomach rolled inside as she thought about this man taking photos and stalking her.

"I hear you," he said, "but stand strong. You're free, and this guy's on the run, and now he's lost his home base too."

"Or his home base is one of many," she said. "I didn't get the feeling that he cared particularly about anything. As if, like I said, he'd done this many times before."

"And that's quite possible," he said. "We just need an ID, and then we can maybe track some more of his movements."

"If he's really stayed to ground all this time," she said, "he could have places like this in multiple cities."

"We believe he may have been doubling up on apartments everywhere."

"That's a huge cost," she muttered.

"And so then we have to consider how he's making his money. How much money does he have?" Nico asked. "Do you know anybody in your world who has that kind of money to do something like this?"

"Of course," she said. "Modeling puts you in touch with all kinds of people. But I don't think I know any who are serial kidnappers or people who would buy another person. But money does funny things to you. I think it can ruin the core of many bad people and even some good ones."

"It doesn't have to," he said with a smile. "In some cases, it allows a good person to help lots of people."

"Then I've met the wrong kind," she said sadly. She shifted in the bed, wincing as her ribs once again screamed at the ache from the movement. "Can you help me lower the bed so I can stretch out for a nap again?" she whispered.

He helped her adjust the bed so it was flatter. "Isn't your sister coming back with coffee?"

"Yes," she said. "I just need to close my eyes for a little bit."

"Good enough," he said. "I've got lots of work here."

"What kind of work?"

"Well, your captor rented that second apartment under the alias John Smith."

That startled a surprising snort out of her. "Well, that's not very original."

"But it obviously works," he said. "Just think about it. The guy managed to rent an apartment."

"But both of them?"

He shook his head. "The other one was a corporation who thought the place was empty."

She stared at him. "Seriously? So, we have a plain thinker, and somebody who likes to keep things simple. He's not creative, and he likes to do things by routine."

Nico's eyebrows shot up. "That's a very good analysis," he said.

"Yeah. I should be a profiler in my next life," she said in a deadpan voice. "Obviously I'm kidding. But he's youngish. Under forty probably and yet has money. He's also very, very efficient."

"How did he move?"

She stared at him in confusion. "I don't know what you mean."

"Did he have a strict military bearing? Was he relaxed? Did he have clipped footsteps?"

"He glided," she said. "Almost couldn't hear his footsteps when I had the blindfold and the earmuffs on. And, when they were off, I kept straining to hear. But there was like nothing to hear. Just a little bit of a sound on the flooring."

"So he was really good at moving in the shadows then?"

"But there was something else. Like an economy of movement, if you understand what I'm trying to say," she said, thinking about it. "No wasted efforts. He didn't, you know, move a muscle or move his hand any farther than was absolutely necessary. So, when I say *efficient*, I mean, he did what he did, and there was no dropping of his hands or waving of his hands, and, when he needed to reach out, he did what he wanted to do and then put his hand away again."

"I've met guys like that," Nico said. "An economy of movement is a good way to describe it."

She smiled and said, "It's what you do when you're hurt or when you're tired. Or at least I do. I preserve every muscle effort, so I do the absolute minimum."

"But some people aren't automatically smooth like that," he said.

"Well, this is one of those guys who are. Yet he never appeared tired. He never appeared to be dragging his feet. He came in, did what he needed, then left."

"Right. But bored?"

"Yes," she said and shared the way he spoke and acted, even the way he'd fed her the sandwich.

"As if he's done this so often that he knew exactly how you'd react."

"Which I think is the only reason why I got away. He didn't expect me to be any different than the other women he's kidnapped," she said slowly. "This guy really needs to be taken out."

"We'll take care of that," he said. "You just close your eyes and sleep. If Ruby returns in the meantime," he said, "she can sit and wait. But chances are, she'll be a little bit yet.”

“Make sure you wake me,” she said. “I don't want to miss seeing her again.”

“I'll wake you,” Nico said. “Just go to sleep.”

She listened to his voice, realizing that she was already three-quarters under. “Good night,” she whispered and let sleep take her deep beneath.

WITH EVERY CUPBOARD and every drawer opened, the authorities found little bits and pieces about who this man was. He didn't cook. There were no dishes other than one plate and one bowl and one cup. *Just to feed his captive, damn him.* There was no cutlery. There was a coffeemaker, and there was instant coffee. “I don't think he lives here full-time either,” Miles said to the detective.

“I agree with that. This is another apartment that he uses for a purpose.”

“There are no laptops, no electronics, no chargers,” he noted when they both stepped into the bedroom. “Why are there no chargers?”

“He probably has a backpack and takes everything with him.”

“I don't know if he had a backpack when Vanessa saw him at street level.”

“Would she have even noticed?” he asked. “She was in a panic, injured and saw him briefly.”

“I know.” He pulled out his phone and sent a text, asking his contact for the video feeds from the sidewalk and if anybody had searched them for a visual on our John Smith, our John Ambrose.

It came back, replying, **Yes, but nothing.**

How can that be?

Not sure.

Miles frowned and put away his phone. "There should be some traffic cam that picks him up. This is a busy intersection."

"Quite true," the detective said. "We've already searched though. And the traffic cam outside this building went down this afternoon. We think it was due to a major accident at the intersection."

"Of course, just around the time that he was here?"

The detective looked at him and nodded.

"What's the chance he's got some handheld device that scrambles the camera feed at the time that he comes close?"

"Well, I sure as hell hope there isn't anything like that," the detective said. "If there is, we're in trouble."

"Chances are not very many people would have access to it anyway," Miles said. "The problem with devices like that is they're often not shared."

"Which is a good thing."

They checked everything they could, and as soon as he was done and the forensic team was called in, Miles handed over his cell phone number to the detective and said, "Let me know what the forensics come back with." And, with that, he disappeared. He headed downstairs and outside, looking for as many cameras around the street area as he could.

If there was a tool out there that disrupted cameras, he wanted to know about it. But it was likely to be some invention that nobody even heard of. It was one thing to have the electronics intact. As he walked around the corner to where Vanessa lived, he called Nico. "So cameras on the street that should have seen the incident and the kidnapper and potentially caught him on film were apparently disabled at the same time."

"How very convenient," Nico said.

"Too convenient," Miles said. "Can you get traffic cam access to the other corners and see if they're all out too? I'm wondering if he has some way of disabling or at least stopping himself from being seen on the cameras."

"Some personal stealth mode?"

"I don't know, but it's weird and a little too coincidental to have the cameras always out at those times. There should be some camera views at every angle. Particularly as this is a main intersection."

"Good point. Did anybody recognize which way he went once he hit that intersection?"

"Go through the witness statements and see if anybody saw him. And what about Vanessa herself? Maybe ask her."

"I will when she wakes up. She's out for the count again."

"Good," Miles said. "Has the doctor been by?"

"Yes. He said she's doing better, but she's to stay overnight, and he'll see her tomorrow."

"I suspect she'll get released tomorrow, and we have to make plans for that."

"Suggestions?"

"At the very minimum, she needs security at her home," he said. "And beyond that, we need to find this guy so he doesn't keep coming after her."

"And the sister?" Nico asked.

"I know. I was thinking of that. If you can't get one, you take the other, right? And then I keep coming back to the fact that if he can get one and there is another, why not take both?"

"That's an ugly thought."

"All of these are ugly thoughts."

"When I was talking to Vanessa earlier," Nico said, "she kept talking about how efficient his movements were, like nothing was wasted. Very economical movement is how she put it."

"Interesting."

"Martial arts could really help to train a person to be like that."

"Great," he said, "as if we don't have enough shit going on. But what else would we expect? She never saw him with any weapon, did she?"

"Wow. I didn't even think to ask her that," Nico said. "Again something to discuss when she wakes up."

"I'm walking around the corner to her place," Miles said. "And taking photos as I go. I highly suspect that this guy will keep an eye on both apartment buildings."

"I would," Nico said. "If nothing else, he'd be afraid of anything he might have left behind."

"He left the photos behind," Miles said. "If those were my photos, I wouldn't be happy. But, if I took the photos, I can always get more printed."

"True enough and from his own printer."

"Except for one thing," Miles said. "No electronics were in that second apartment at all."

At that, Nico whistled lightly. "So you think he has a third place?"

"I think he has to have someplace that he calls home, too far away to bother driving back and forth, so he keeps this place because it's convenient and because that's where his prisoner is."

"So, what's too far to drive?"

"And that's another thing. Do we even know if he drives?"

"Odds are he does," Nico said. "I think you know the percentages would say that he does."

"So, is an hour one way too far? If so, then we need to determine a radius and see how many of these women disappeared an hour away from London."

"I can do that. I'll start with that parameter, then widen it if necessary," he said. "Gives me something to do while she's sleeping."

"Okay, I'll do a full sweep on her apartment, and then I'll come back in." And he hung up.

CHAPTER 9

VANESSA WOKE UP to see her sister sitting there quietly beside her.

"Hey, sleepyhead."

She smiled, then murmured, "Did you bring coffee?"

"Sure did," she said. "Not much good it is if you're sleeping though."

"I'll still drink it cold," she said.

"Don't have to. I just got in."

With her sister's help, she shifted in the bed so she was sitting up more, and then, when the pain finally eased, she relaxed into the multiple pillows and smiled up at her bright and cheerful younger sister. "How were things out there?"

"Completely normal," she said. "It's as if nobody has any idea there's this dark underbelly that thrives in a metropolis like our city."

"All cities are like that," Nico said from the side. "People only live in the upper half. Nobody ever wants to descend and see what's happening in the underbelly of society."

"Of course not," Ruby said. "It's ugly down there."

He nodded, his tone serious. "It is, indeed. But it's that darkness, that ugliness, that creeps from the underside up into your world."

"So how do we get rid of the entire underbelly?" Vanessa asked with interest. "I've been touched twice by it now, and I really don't want to have a third encounter." She watched his face, but he didn't show any signs of understanding what she was talking about, so maybe Miles hadn't shared what had happened to her as a child.

"I'm not sure there's any way to avoid it," he said, "and I think, if you fear it, it attracts it."

"Probably," she said. "But I'm lying here thinking about the options of moving to a new place, and I really don't like that. We were really proud and happy when we bought that apartment."

Ruby nodded.

"Do you know your neighbors?" Nico asked the sisters.

"I can tell you that my captor is not one of them," Vanessa said with a laugh. "I'd certainly recognize him, if that were the case."

"Me too," Ruby added.

"But considering that he owns multiple apartments not very far away from you, and you didn't know …"

Vanessa wrinkled her nose up at him. "That's hardly fair."

"Remember. This isn't about fairness," he said. "This is about finding the asshole who did this to you."

A hard knock came on the door, and then it opened immediately.

She watched as Miles stepped toward her. Her heart jumped, and, even as she recognized it was him, her hands reached for him. He grabbed her fingers and leaned over, then kissed her gently on the cheek while she hugged him. "I told you that I'd come back," he whispered.

She smiled, nodded and sank back. "You did, indeed. A man of his word. I like that."

"Good," he said with a soft smile. "How are you feeling?"

She could see his gaze running over her features and down her hands and arms. "I'm fine," she said a little too firmly.

"Well, you're improving. We'll go with that."

"Okay," she said. "It's just so hard to believe he had two apartments."

"And I just came from your apartment," he said. "Interesting place."

"I could have met you there," Ruby said, "and given you a tour."

"And maybe we'll do that later," he said. "I wanted to see the size, the views and how many people were about. Things like that."

"And did you go to the little grassy space in the back?" Ruby asked.

He nodded. "It's a nice little area."

"It used to be," Ruby said. "But an asshole watching me as I sat there and stalking me will not make me go back again."

"Good," he said. "In daylight, it's probably not a bad idea. But it's never a good idea to make your actions habitual."

"But that's because we don't think like you," Vanessa said. "How can we? It's just way too dark a viewpoint. We don't want to live like that."

"Maybe, but it doesn't change the fact that somebody targeted you."

"Because of the color of my hair," she said in disgust. "That makes no sense."

Miles turned to look at Nico. "Did you get that mapped out?"

"Yes," he said. "And it's pretty interesting." He opened up his laptop and clicked a few times and then swiveled it so that Miles could see. He walked over and lifted it up to take a look and saw at least eight dots within that circle.

"So, if he's using this as a central base," he said, "then there has to be some other place here that's even closer."

"That's what I was wondering," Nico said. "Eight of them just in this circle. So, eight redheads were taken within this general area around London. And they're all fairly scattered."

He nodded. "What about the other nine? Did you map them?"

"Here's a map of all seventeen that we have figured out so far. And now, of course, one has escaped."

Miles shot her a special smile at that.

She could feel her heart warming, knowing she'd done something that he really approved of. Hell, she approved of it too. She shouldn't be looking for his approval, but it was really nice to see how proud he was of her for managing to escape this psycho. She motioned at the laptop. "May I take a look at that, please?"

Miles nodded and carried the laptop over, noting each of the red dots located on the map. "It's not something you think about," she said, "but seeing a visual like this …"

"I'm still struggling as to why you guys didn't possibly figure this out before," Ruby said.

"Remember, Ruby," Vanessa said. "These guys just came on the job."

Ruby nodded. "So are the police always that slow?"

"No," Nico said, "because, just within this last hour, we've determined the seventeen women were in different counties and different districts. Sure, there's a database of crimes, but it's not shared with all law officers. And not everybody's on it, and not everybody reports everything, and, over one single year, one missing redhead is not a pattern."

"No, it's not," Vanessa said. "And this dot would have been one woman for some particular year, and then another dot is one for another year, correct?" As she tapped the first one and then another, she watched Miles and Nico nod. "So who noted the similarity in the pattern?"

Miles pointed at Nico.

"But I thought you guys just came on the case?"

Miles nodded. "But Nico worked for MI5 before and then, on special assignment later, had another case in Paris that was similar to this, and it made him take another look. That's when he found the pattern. Then brought me in to help."

"Wow," Vanessa said, looking over at Nico. "Too bad you weren't on the job seventeen years ago."

"I can't judge anybody who was on the job all these years," Nico said. "It's a very difficult pattern just to find. Also, even though we know it's a pattern now, it's damn hard to pinpoint the kidnapper." He glanced over at Miles. "What about the video cameras?"

"I have to check in with the team because it makes no sense. Apparently our guy is either lucky, or he has a way of controlling the street cameras."

"True, or maybe he has some software that just blurs the pixels," he said.

"I don't know," Vanessa said. "He has a hat and a beard, so it's pretty darn easy for him to change his appearance from one camera to the next."

He looked at her in surprise and laughed and said, "You're right. It could be just that easy." He brought up the video cameras. "While you guys have your coffee, I'll sit here with Nico, and we'll look again."

"He didn't have any of those disguises on outside on the street when I first escaped," she said.

"Until he went around a corner," he said, "and then he could have added a hat or a beard. He could have changed shirts or just took off one. Considering the number of years he could have been doing this—he could have learned to use any number of disguises."

"A master of disguise." She thought about it and then nodded. "That fits. There was something very efficient about him."

"I remember you saying that," he said. "And, of course, it doesn't take very much after you've done this a few times."

Just then his phone rang.

"THERE'S A MATCH on the fingerprints," the detective said.

"Seriously?" Miles said. "That's good news. What do we have?"

He hesitated and then said, "A dead man." And hung up.

Miles turned slowly to look at Nico. "The fingerprints in the second apartment belong to a dead man."

Nico's frown was instantaneous. "Shit," he said.

Miles nodded. "We're getting the information coming through by email now." Just then his phone beeped to say it was in. He shifted to the laptop, brought it up and said, "Look at that. So we have a dead man who died supposedly six years ago."

"He's been very careful to not leave fingerprints anywhere," Nico said.

"Yeah. This was on a lightbulb apparently. When he changed the bulb in the bedroom."

Nico laughed. "Not exactly something that anybody is thinking about when they change a lightbulb."

"So, if this dead man isn't who he says he is, then the question is, did our guy here kill this man and make it look like it was him or what? Unless, of course, it was his apartment first."

At that, Nico winced. "That's possible too. I'll bring up the purchase and the deed on the place."

While Nico worked on his laptop, Miles checked out the information on that fingerprint. Apparently the man died in a car accident, and his body was badly burned. So, was it really him who died, or was it somebody else? If he had owned the apartment at any point in time or had visited the apartment, that's a different story. He did have a rap sheet of breaking and entering and petty theft though. So it's possible that the dead man and Ambrose were associates. But it didn't mean that Vanessa's imprisonment involved the dead man.

"So, look at that," Nico said. "He was the owner of that second apartment twelve years ago."

"And that lightbulb," Miles said, "may not have been changed out in the last six years?"

"It's possible, especially if he was not there very long, and the place was vacant for a long time. Or was it one of those long-life LED bulbs? Those last for years."

"Shit," Miles said, "so maybe it's not him." And when Miles's phone rang again, he said, "Yes, what's up?"

"Two other fingerprints. This time it's a different man."

"Good, because the fingerprint that you found on the lightbulb matched the owner of that apartment, who bought the place twelve years ago and apparently died in a car accident six years ago."

"Right. We did figure that out ourselves. Now these two fingerprints are a different story."

"Where did you find them?"

"Under the toilet seat."

"Interesting," he said, frowning. "And who do they belong to?"

"Damon Stahl," he said. "I'm sending you the information. He's wanted in Europe."

"Wanted for what?"

"Kidnapping, sexual offenses, sex trade."

"Wow. That sounds like our man then," he said.

"Yep, that's what I'm thinking. We have an image that I've forwarded to you."

"I'm waiting for it to come through now," he said. And, sure enough, it came up on his laptop. He brought up the picture and whistled. "That's him," he said. "That's definitely him." He flipped his laptop around and held it up for Vanessa to see from the bed. The color stripped away from her face, and she nodded. "Yes, that's him."

"Did you hear that? That's Vanessa confirming it."

"Good. Damon Stahl. So our John Ambrose has reinvented himself as Damon Stahl, John Smith and Barry White," he said. "That's the man we want. Unfortunately he's been wanted for ten years."

"Ten years in Europe?"

"Yes, and he's relatively unheard of over here."

"So, what's with the seventeen years of the women disappearing?"

"Who knows?" he said. "The warrant outstanding for the European community is ten years old, so he was over there being very active and then came over here and went underground."

"Great. So, if he's supplying women for the sex trade, he could have been doing that over there a little more openly until the warrant was issued a decade ago. So he began fishing from this part of the world since then? And then he had to go underground and be a whole lot quieter over here while fishing."

"Yes," the detective said. "We don't have any family or next of kin. Nothing."

"No. He has no living blood relatives, since he was like one year old. Adopted at twelve. So, we have an alias and a face and his fingerprint. What about DNA?"

"They're checking it," he said. "There wasn't very much in the way of forensic evidence in either of the apartments."

"No, he's a pro," Miles said. "But even pros make mistakes."

"Well, he's made one now," the detective said. "We got his fingerprints. And that puts him in both apartments. So now we have a much better idea of what he's doing."

"Not to mention that it's kitty-corner to where Vanessa and her sister lived."

"Yes, we brought that up in the map too. We have mapped all seventeen of the missing redheads in relation to that double set of apartments. It doesn't make sense that he kidnapped all those people and kept them there, but it's a good system."

"He could also quite probably have at least one more location."

"And why is that?" asked the detective, his voice almost distracted.

"No electronics," he said. "No printer for those photos,

no chargers, nothing."

"Right. So we're still looking for another property, where he actually lives."

"Search under his name and his aliases. I know it's a big stretch, but …"

"Already in progress," he said. "I'll let you know if we find anything."

"Okay," and they hung up.

"So, interestingly enough, we have a new name, a face and a confirmed ID. We're setting up an alert for anybody to approach cautiously." Miles looked at Vanessa. "Did you ever see a weapon?"

She shook her head. "*He* was the weapon. I figured he would snap my neck like a twig," she said.

"That muscled?"

She nodded. "That big, that muscled and that dead inside."

"Good to know," he said. "And did he ever have a backpack with him?"

"He did out on the street," she said and nodded. "But I don't think it was all that big."

"No, but it'll have his essentials," he said. "Now we just have to be lucky enough to track him down."

"Facial recognition is in progress, scouring the city for him," Nico said. "So far, nothing."

"They'll have to run more than one photo, some with the hats and some with a beard."

"You know that trying to find somebody who can change disguises like that won't be easy."

"No," Miles said, "not at all. But it's not impossible. What we need to know is if he has European connections. Would he take a chance of going over there again?"

"Not if Interpol's after him. That's quite likely a place he'd avoid."

"Scotland? Ireland? Or change locations altogether and just walk away from this one because it's now a bad deal?"

"That's what he's more likely to do," Nico said, "because he's got an awful lot invested here."

"He's also really angry," Vanessa interrupted. "He won't let this go. He'll come after me again."

"Think so?"

"Oh, yeah," she said. "He's already figuring out how to get to me."

Miles looked over at her and smiled. "Well, let him figure it out, and then I'll be waiting."

CHAPTER 10

THE REST OF the evening passed so quickly between naps and long periods of sleep, waking to go to the bathroom, eating and then sleeping some more. By the time Vanessa woke the next morning, she almost felt normal again. As she shifted to get out of the bed, Miles hopped up once again to help her.

"I'm getting much better, you know," she said good-naturedly.

"Good," he said. "I'm glad to hear that."

"Did you get any sleep last night?"

"I got some," he said, "but I kept thinking that we would have an intruder."

"Me too," she said. "I kept waking up to make sure I could see you, and I'd fall back asleep again."

He chuckled. "Happy to help."

"I don't know what I'll do without you though," she said.

"Not an issue," he said. "I'm not going anywhere until we find this guy."

"Promise?" She was at the bathroom door and about to close it, when he hesitated. She frowned up at him. "Promise?" she repeated.

He gave a clipped nod. "I promise."

She smiled, closed the door and made good use of the

bathroom for yet another time. All those trips to the bathroom went unnoticed when she was healthy. But each painful trip now was duly noted. And, when she opened it again, he still stood there, waiting for her. She made it back to the bed, walking much easier, and said, "I'd really like to go home today."

"When the doctor comes around for his rounds, we'll see if that's possible."

"Do you think I should though?" She sank back down on the bed and stared up at him. "Or is that just foolish?"

"It's both," he said cheerfully. "But it's your home. It's your natural surroundings, so, of course, you want to go home. You won't go alone."

"My sister?"

"I imagine she'll want to go home too."

"Well, she didn't want to go to her friend's house last night. I know that."

"Well, until this is a done deal," he said, "we have to be as smart about our actions as we can."

"Do you think he'll attack me at home?"

"As long as I'm there, I'd like to think so," he said. "But, with us around, it may be too much of a military presence for him to want to tackle it."

As she sat on the bed, stretching and easing some of her stiff muscles, she asked, "Are you moving in then?"

"I'm definitely staying with you," he said. "We'll see how that works out."

Her phone rang then. She looked at it and frowned. "Ruby, why are you calling so early?"

"I wanted to go home last night, but then I decided that you're right, and I should go to Mark's house. So, I'm still over at Mark's, but I want to get a change of clothes. Do you think it's okay?"

She looked at Miles. "Ruby wants to get a change of clothing from home."

"If she can wait until we get there," he said, "it would be better."

She relayed the message to Ruby.

Hearing her sister sigh heavily, she reminded her, "Don't forget what happened to me."

"I can hardly forget that," she said and hung up.

At that, she twisted and looked at Miles and said, "Did you ever get a hold of my cousin?"

He shook his head. "No answer at his door and he didn't answer his phone."

"Seriously?"

He nodded.

She pulled out her phone, searched her contacts and hit her cousin's contact number.

When he answered the phone, she said, "Hey, Tristan. A special investigator was trying to get a hold of you yesterday and the day before." She listened to his surprised voice on the other end. "Something about your visits to the apartment in the last year or so." He snorted at that. "Do you mind if he talks to you now?"

"No, I have to go to work," he said. "What's this all about?"

She put it on Speakerphone, and Miles leaned forward. "I don't know if you know, but your cousin was kidnapped the day before yesterday and escaped yesterday morning," he said. "So we're looking into all aspects of her life."

"Oh, my God," Tristan said. "Vanessa, are you okay?"

"Yeah, I'm fine," she said. "But it was a pretty rough ride. So they caught sight of you around my apartment twice. Ruby says she talked to you one of those two times, but the other time you were standing there, staring at the apartment."

He groaned. "Yeah, that figures that they'd catch sight of that," he said. "I kept thinking that, if I asked you for a meeting with one of your photographers, then maybe I could get into modeling faster. But then you know that because I sent you an email about it."

"But you didn't come up to the apartment, and you just waited?"

"I was waiting for you to come home," he said. "But you never did."

"When was that?"

"A few weeks ago," he said, stifling a yawn audibly through the phone. "I think you were traveling, but I didn't realize it at the time. I think I was there a couple other times as well. But honestly it was nothing nefarious. I just wanted to see if there was any chance of you giving me a hand up."

"And did you give up on that idea?" she asked curiously.

"I looked into a different modeling job," he said sheepishly. "And I didn't want to say anything in case it didn't go anywhere."

"That's wonderful," she said in surprise. "You should do really well with it."

"I don't know about that," he said. "It's small bananas at the moment, and I'll see what I can do with it."

"Exactly," she said warmly. "Just keep trying. You never know when something will break."

"Well, that's the idea," he said, laughing. "Anyway I hope that explains the reasons for my visits."

"Absolutely," Miles said. "I'm sending you a photo. I want to see if you recognize the man. Call me back as soon as you get it." And they hung up the call, and Miles quickly sent the picture of Ambrose, and Tristan called back immediately.

"You know what? That's really weird because I saw him one of the times that I was there waiting. He came up and talked to me. I think it was the last time I was there, just a few weeks ago."

"What?" Vanessa asked. "What do you mean, he talked to you?"

"Yeah. He said that he was waiting for his girlfriend to come back from a trip, and he noticed me hanging around."

"So, he was acting like you were stalking his girlfriend?" Miles asked, lunging forward so he could get closer to the phone.

"Yeah, that's kind of the way it was, yeah," Tristan said. "Who is this guy?"

"The guy who held me captive," she said.

"Weird," he said. "And holy crap, I actually talked to this guy."

"Did you see where he went, or did he say anything about the apartment he was in?" Miles asked.

"He just pointed up toward your apartment, Vanessa," he said. "But he was pointing to the building, not necessarily to your apartment."

"And he didn't say anything else? He didn't give the name of the girl?" Miles asked.

Tristan thought about it for a moment and said, "I don't think so, but he might have said Beth. I can't remember."

"Thanks. If you think of anything else, let me know," Miles said.

"Yeah, well," he said, worried now, "I'm not in any danger, am I?"

"I don't think so," Vanessa said. "But this guy is still on the loose, so, if you see him, let us know."

"And stay away from him," Miles reiterated.

"Will do." Tristan suddenly hung up.

When the phone went dead, Miles looked over at her. "Do you trust your cousin?"

"I have no reason not to," she said.

"So you think he really has a modeling gig?"

"I wouldn't be at all surprised," she said. "When you see him up close, he's got really high cheekbones and super-flaxen skin. The camera will love him," she said.

"Interesting. Well, okay then," he said. "We'll knock him down the list a little bit."

At that, she groaned. "Is everybody in my world suspect?"

"Until this nightmare is over, everybody is suspect."

"Fine," she said. "So now what?"

Just then the door opened, and the doctor walked in. "There we go," he said. "You're looking better already."

Miles excused himself as the doctor did a very thorough physical, standing at the doorway to the bathroom with his back turned.

When she was finally covered up again, she winced from the pain. "What about it, Doctor? Do I get to go home?"

"Well, I can't say I'd be unhappy to get the security guard out of here," he said. "But I only want you to go home if you'll be careful when you're there. We don't want you coming back here even more injured."

"Believe me. I'm not trying to," she said with a smile. "And I'll have bodyguards coming with me too."

"Perfect," he said. "In that case, I'll give you clearance to go home." Then he smiled, shook her hand and took his leave.

When Miles turned around, he had a big grin on his face. "Well, now you should be happy."

"Absolutely," she said. "But I don't have any clothes."

"Well," he said. "We're not far from your place. I'll head over. You need to have breakfast and some coffee anyway, and you probably need to wait on the final paperwork and have the nurses do their final rounds. So, I can be back in what? Half an hour? Forty minutes?"

She nodded. "A shower would be good too, before I leave. Or maybe one at home?" She was undecided.

He lifted a hand and said, "I'll get Nico to come in and sit with you."

"Is Nico around?"

He nodded. "He was on watch at the hospital, just in case."

She shook her head. "But you guys didn't get any sleep?"

"We did," he said. "In four-hour shifts."

She watched as Miles made a phone call, and then, within a few minutes, Nico walked in with a big grin on his face. "So you are getting out of here, are you?"

She smiled and said, "Yeah. Are you okay to sit and watch over me while Miles gets me some clothes?"

"I can do that easily enough," he said, "especially if we'll get coffee delivered." He looked over at the Miles. "Why don't you bring up that chat box and order us some real food for breakfast?"

Miles rolled his eyes. "Fine. I can do that. And then I'll be back real fast."

He sent the text and then headed out, and it wasn't ten minutes before another knock came on Vanessa's hospital room door. Nico immediately hopped up and answered the door and then brought in a trolley. He smiled and led it over to the bed. And while she watched, he lifted the lids and uncovered coffee and fresh bagels and what looked like scrambled eggs.

She grinned. "Okay, at least we can eat while he's gone." And then he grabbed the first plate and placed it on a small table for her and brought her some coffee.

"The second plate's for me," he said. "Unless you're super-hungry?"

"Go on and eat," she said. "I can't believe you guys stayed up all night."

He shrugged and moved the trolley back out into the hallway, then took a look. She could see his gaze going up and down the hallway before he closed the door. "Nobody there?"

He shook his head. "Nobody is there." An odd note was in his voice, and he typed something on his phone.

"Then what about that bothers you?" She picked up a piece of toasted bagel, melted butter dripping all down the side, and took a big bite. She moaned. "Oh, my gosh, this is so good."

He nodded, but his face was troubled.

She realized he hadn't answered her question. "What's the matter?"

"The guard's not there," he said briefly. "I've notified hospital security."

She frowned at that and shrugged, then said, "I imagine they need a shift change too."

"I know," he said. "He was there when I came in though."

"So then Miles said something to him," she said, ignoring it. She trusted these guys to keep her safe. She munched happily on her bagel for a few moments, finishing that off, and then dug into her scrambled eggs. By the time she was done with all the food, she was stunned that her plate was empty. "Okay," she said. "I was hungrier than I expected to be."

"It's all good," he said. "Do you want some of mine?"

She shook her head. "No, I'm fine now. But I'll have my coffee."

He nodded and handed it to her. She leaned back and sipped it, then said, "Are you coming to the apartment with me too?"

"In between helping look after you and trying to track down this guy, we'll be switching off on a regular basis."

She nodded. "Good, because I certainly don't want to be alone right now."

"No," he said. "Of course you don't." He picked up his phone and sent a text.

Because he'd been acting a little bit odd, she said, "What was that about?"

He looked at her and flashed her a bright smile. "What makes you think I was doing anything?"

"You were typing."

"I was just checking to make sure Miles had spoken to the guard before he left."

"And?"

"I haven't heard back," he said with a shrug. Then he picked up his coffee and studied it. "Is this hospital coffee?"

"I doubt it," she said. "It tastes too good. So did the bagel."

"It's hard to mess up a toasted bagel," he said.

She laughed at that. "I agree, but this is delicious," she said as she took another sip. When forty-five minutes had gone by, she kept checking with Nico to see what time it was and was now checking on her phone too. "So, where is he?"

"You worried about Miles?" Nico asked curiously. "Or are you just anxious to go home?"

She flushed. "Of course I'm worried about him. A dangerous man is out there."

"Don't kid yourself," he said. "Miles is up for any of those challenges. He's probably way more dangerous than your kidnapper."

She stared at him in surprise. "He doesn't look the type," she said slowly.

He smiled at her. "Remember how you thought your kidnapper could be very angry? Miles doesn't waste effort with being angry. He just gets even."

She smiled. "I like the sound of that. Hopefully he's found my bloody kidnapper, and he's beaten him to a pulp," she said. But, when Miles didn't show up another fifteen minutes later, she really got worried. "Where is he?" she cried out. "How do you know that he isn't injured in a back alley somewhere?"

"I don't," he said. "I can send a patrol car to your apartment, if you want though."

She nodded immediately. "Yes, please do." He nodded and quickly brought out his phone and sent a text. She looked at him. "Is that it? That's all you have to do? Send a text?"

"Yes," he said, looking at her carefully. "Why?"

"Well, why didn't you send one to Miles earlier?"

His voice was low and hard when he answered, "I did, and I didn't get any answer."

MILES WALKED THROUGH the apartment and collected a small bag, then considered what to bring as a change of clothing for her. He wasn't sure what she would like, but it was a warm day, so he figured that, considering she had stacks of leggings and long tunics, maybe he could get away with a simple pair of those. He grabbed some underclothes and a pair of soft ballet shoes, then had them in a bag and was just about to exit the apartment when he heard something off.

He immediately hid behind the door and waited. But there was nothing. Nobody came in. He didn't like the sound of that because it didn't sound so much like a door opening as much as the door opening, closing, opening and closing. He would put that down to somebody making it sound like several people had entered the apartment across from him. He didn't know why it bugged him. It just didn't sound right. It sounded fake, almost like a kid standing there, opening and closing the door.

With everything in the apartment as he had left it, he opened the door and stepped out, closing it immediately behind him. The hallway around was deserted. He frowned, wondering what he'd heard. He was not somebody who ignored his instincts, and, at this point in time, they prodded him that something was wrong. He stuffed her clothes into his pocket, having to shove the bag in tight to get it in there. He chose everything that was super flimsy and light, so it was pretty easy to squeeze in. And then, with his hands free, he walked down to the end of the hallway to where the exit was. He headed outside to make sure nobody was there and then stepped back inside to see if anybody was following him. A double set of doors were between the exit doors, so that he could wait in between to see if anybody came down the hallway.

After five minutes, he figured it was safe, and he peered around the corner to see a man coming out of the apartment across from hers. He walked across and tested the lock on Vanessa's door, and, when he found it was locked and wouldn't open, he bent to see if he could work with something in his hand to pick it open. Immediately Miles opened the double door and raced toward him, yelling, "Hey, asshole."

The guy took one look and bolted, but Miles was already running. The guy made it out the front door but hit a wall of people heading for work. Miles grabbed him and tossed him onto the grass in the front lawn, then hit him once and knocked him down. Immediately they were surrounded by a crowd of people, protesting his behavior. He glanced at them and held up his badge. There were still a few insults, like police brutality, but he shook his head and quickly tied the guy up and called for the detective. When the detective answered the phone, Miles explained what had happened.

"The guy was trying to get into Vanessa's apartment?"

"Yeah. I don't know if he was just a robber or if he knew she was out of the apartment. It's not the guy we're looking for."

"Of course not," he said in that exaggerated heavy voice. "I'll send somebody down to pick him up."

Miles helped the guy stand up and then said, "You always break into women's apartments?"

The guy glared at him and didn't say anything.

"That's fine," he said. "That one was just kidnapped. We're more than happy to pin you to that case."

Immediately the guy's eyes opened wide. "Hey, hey! I don't know anything about that," he said. "It's got nothing to do with me."

"So, what were you doing trying to break into her apartment?"

"I wasn't," he said. "There was just an odd design on the doorknob, and I was taking a closer look."

"I don't think so. I know exactly what you were doing, and so do you."

The guy glared at him. "So what? I knew she was in the hospital. So chances were, the place was empty, and I could scope it out."

"So you engage in a little bit of B&E of people already struggling, is that it? You wait until somebody has a catastrophe, and you go in and clean out their place?"

"Well, what the hell," he said. "I knew two women lived there. For all I knew, the sister was there too."

"But then you wouldn't have gone in, would you?"

The guy glared at him.

"Unless of course, you're stalking the sister too."

At that, the guy started backing away. "Hey, man, no. I don't have anything to do with that."

"So, how did you know the sister wasn't here?" Something was odd about this guy's expression. As Miles turned to glance around the crowd, he caught a glimpse of some man getting in the rear passenger side of a vehicle, staring at him sideways, sunglasses and a hat on. And Miles realized it was the kidnapper. Miles swore and shouted, but the guy's driver gunned it and took off. He turned to look at his B&E guy and said, "He paid you, didn't he?"

Immediately the guy froze. "I don't know what you're talking about," he said hurriedly.

"That guy'll kill you for getting caught," Miles threatened.

"No, no, no, no," he said. "He's not like that."

"Really? But he hired you to break into this woman's apartment?"

"Well, he told me that it was a good opportunity. The place was empty. That's all," he said.

"Why did he do you such a favor?"

The guy shrugged and didn't say anything.

"Speak up now before things get nasty."

"Because I help him out every once in a while."

"Yeah, with what?"

The guy glared at him but fell silent.

"It's okay," Miles said. "I'll find out, and I'll turn your life upside down. I'll dig into your friends, your job, your bank accounts, … and, if there are any irregularities, we'll nail your ass to the wall."

"Hey, you've got no right to do any of that," he said.

"Sure I do," he said. "Where do you work?"

"I'm a programmer," he said.

"With a steady job?"

The guy glared at him.

"So that translates to being a hacker, huh?"

"Maybe," he said. "But I don't do anything wrong. I play games mostly."

"And," Miles said, "shut down traffic cameras when it's convenient, huh?"

At that, the guy's eyes widened in panic, and he backed away, but Miles wasn't letting him take even a step.

"No, no, no," he said. "We'll have a nice little talk with you."

"Hell no," he said. "You want that guy. Go after him."

"I already know what vehicle he's driving," Miles said. "And the traffic cameras, without you erasing them right now, will give us exactly where he went."

The guy panicked. "I don't know anything about that," he cried out.

"Yeah, you do. You know an awful lot, and I need to know everything you know."

"There's nothing to say," he said.

"You better talk. Otherwise we'll just nail your ass for seventeen kidnappings over seventeen years."

At that, the guy started to blubber. "Hey, I don't have anything to do with that."

"So, what's your deal with this guy who just took off?"

His hacker thief fell silent, and then he shrugged and said, "He pays me every once a while. I kind of need it for rent."

"And what is he paying you to do?"

"Sometimes to pick up food. Sometimes to shut down traffic cameras. Sometimes, you know, I don't know," he said. "Just odd jobs."

"And how does he pay you?"

"Cash," he said.

"How does he contact you?"

"On my phone," he said. "It's in my pocket."

Miles fished it from his pocket and unlocked it as per the guy's instructions and then said, "Which one's him?"

And he scrolled through the contacts. "There, the unknown one."

"And you never called him?"

"I have a couple times, when I couldn't pick up whatever it was that he really wanted."

"Well, that's helpful," he said. "What number?"

He hesitated, and Miles just gave him a hard shake. "The cops are on the way, but you need to tell me exactly what's going on here because this guy kidnapped another woman, and I want to know where he lives."

"He's close," he said.

"Where do you deliver the food to?"

"Just around the corner."

Miles swore at that. "Just around what corner?"

And this time, he pointed across the block. "In those apartments over there."

He stared at him in shock and looked back to where he pointed. "Show me," and he dragged him across the street, following his instructions. "And what's your name?"

"Ross. Ross McMurray," he said. "Look. I couldn't get a full-time job, so I do odd jobs for him. That's all I do."

"Keep walking. I want to know exactly where you deliver that food to."

They were now at the corner. Turning right led to Ambrose's apartment where they'd found Vanessa, but instead Ross led Miles in the opposite direction. They stopped in front of an old brick building, of which there are a million just like it in London. And Ross said, "In here." He led the way inside. "Up on the second floor." And they went up to the second floor, and then he pointed out the door.

Immediately Miles called for backup.

The detective said, "My guys are looking for you. Where the hell are you?"

Miles answered, "I've got the kidnapper's delivery boy here. We're at apartment number two forty two," and he gave the street address. "I want backup right now because we're going in and taking a look."

"Give me five," the detective said. "I'm only a couple blocks away."

He leaned Ross up against the wall and said, "What else

do you know about this guy?"

"Nothing," he said. "He's an oddity, that's all. Does weird things and I don't really understand it."

"Interesting. Well, this is your one chance. I suggest you tell me anything that will help us to capture this guy."

"I don't know. I gave you his place and his phone number. Isn't that enough?"

"Have you ever been inside this apartment?"

He nodded. "Yeah, I have. But, well, just in the front. I never got a chance to walk on in."

"Was he ever with anybody?"

He shook his head. "No, he meets his business partners elsewhere."

"And where is that?"

"Another apartment down around the corner," he said. "Just back the other way."

"And why does he meet them there?"

He shrugged. "I don't know why the dude does business this way," he said. "I'm just trying to make a living."

"Well, we'll see what kind of living you get to make now," he said.

Just then the police officers bolted up the stairs toward them.

Miles nodded and said, "This is the door."

"We're going in." Immediately the officers drew their weapons and broke down the door. Shots were immediately fired from inside.

Miles glanced at Ross and asked, "Are you sure he lives alone?"

"Yeah," he said, cringing on the floor. "Shit. I don't want to get shot."

But the cops looked inside and noted that it was empty.

The door had been rigged to fire as soon as somebody entered. "This place was rigged." They came back to Miles. "We need to go in carefully."

"You hold him," Miles said. "I'll take a look." And, with them hanging on to Ross, and the detective on his way, Miles took a slow, deep breath and entered. He crouched low, seeing tripwires all over the place, and pulled a multi-tool from his pocket and carefully snipped the wires. He didn't see anything wired to blow, but more were wired to shoot. After clearing out three tripwires and making it through each of the few rooms inside, he called out to the front and said, "I think you're good to go."

"Do you think so?"

"Well, I've taken out three tripwires, but it's anybody's guess."

One of the detectives walked to the window and said, "Son of a bitch. This place is a nightmare." And just then a single shot rang out, coming through the glass and striking the detective's shoulder right in front of Miles. Immediately the cops were on the run after the shooter, and the second detective who had just arrived took off as well.

Miles checked the officer's wound and said, "Good thing it's just the shoulder." The officer nodded. Swearing, Miles carefully studied outside the window; the shooter had to be in the opposite building. Then Miles raced out to the hallway to see Ross still cringing in the corner. "Well, Ross, you got yourself into a fine mess," he snapped. He grabbed the man's arm roughly. "Come on into the apartment."

"Hell no," he said. "People are dying in there."

"Well, I'm not leaving you alone out here," Miles said. "So, you better come with me and sit still." He went in to find the detective swearing and holding his bloody shoulder.

"We've already got an ambulance on the way. Let's keep you both below the window."

"Who is the guy who lives here?" the detective whispered.

Ross answered. "He's one freaky dude."

"Do you know his name?"

"Well, the name he used was John Smith. But there ain't nobody called John Smith in today's age."

Miles thought about that and nodded. "Maybe not. But hopefully this is the apartment we're looking for."

"He's got tons of apartments. He moves packages. He's a delivery man."

"Yeah, he does," Miles said. "But those *packages* he moves are women."

Ross's eyes widened, and he shook his head. "No. No way. I'm not part of that shit."

"Well, you better offer something decent for us to believe you," Miles said, "because now your buddy is involved in shooting a detective."

"That wasn't me," he said. "You guys already had me."

"What do you know about the women? And don't lie to me."

"I don't know anything about women. Well, I know he lost one. Or one package. He lost a package, and he was pissed."

"When did you talk to him last?"

"This morning," he said.

That's when Miles realized why this guy was breaking into Vanessa's apartment. "You weren't trying to break in to steal something. You were trying to break in to leave something." He got up and held out his hand. "Hand it over."

Ross shrugged and said, "I can't. My hands are tied."

"What is it that *John Smith* wants in there?" Miles asked, checking Ross's pockets. Miles pulled out an audio listening device. "Really? You would bug her apartment?"

Ross sagged in place and nodded. "Yeah, but I didn't realize what for."

"Sure, you did. You set this up so this guy could come and kidnap that poor woman all over again. What kind of bastard are you?"

CHAPTER 11

WHEN HER CLOTHES arrived via a police officer instead of Miles himself, she dressed quickly in the bathroom and stood at the door to her hospital room, impatiently waiting for Nico to pack up his stuff.

"If I'd realized you were in such a hurry," he murmured, "I'd have gotten ready a while ago."

"Something's wrong," she said. "I don't know what it is, but it's something else." And because she seemed to be in a hurry, he seemed to be going as slow as molasses.

Finally he stepped in front of her and opened the door. "Let's go then."

As they stepped outside, the guard looked at her in surprise. She smiled. "I've been sprung free, so I think that means your job's over with."

He shook his head. "Perfect. Glad to see a happy ending here." And he turned and headed down the hallway.

They exited the hospital, but, even then, she felt everybody was going super slowly. She was moving as fast as she could, but it was still not fast enough because of her ankle. Although it felt much better, and she could put weight on it, she was still forced to use crutches or a wheelchair. Doctor's orders. But it was amazing just how fast she could motor down the hallway on crutches. She just had to be mindful of her sore ribs. She didn't particularly like crutches, but, if it meant getting back to her apartment and finding out whatever was going on with Miles, she would use them.

When they finally got outside, she stopped and looked at Nico. "Do we need to take a cab?"

He shook his head and pointed at an SUV, Miles hopping out.

She cried out, "There you are. I was so worried about you." That stopped him in his tracks. She flushed, not realizing just how emotional seeing him again would be.

But he walked over and wrapped her up gently in his arms, then held her. She burrowed in deep, loving the fact that he didn't even ask questions or make a snide comment but understood that she was desperate for that contact. When she realized that the others were probably having a hell of a good old look, she stepped back slowly and smiled up at him. "Glad to see you're okay."

"I'm okay," he said. "We had a bit of interesting action." Instantly she reached out to check that he was all right. He grabbed her hands and tucked her up close again, then murmured against her ear, "I'm fine."

And finally realizing he meant it, and he wasn't hurt or hiding any serious wounds, she relaxed. "Well, I'm glad to hear that," she said, trying for a more neutral tone of voice. But when he grinned, his grin told her that he wasn't in any way fooled. She flushed again. "So, is it safe to go back to my apartment?"

"Did you get my earlier message?" Miles asked Nico instead of answering her.

Nico nodded. "Techs should be at the apartment right now."

"Techs for what?" she asked.

"Do you know a guy named Ross?" He pulled out his

phone and quickly flicked through until he found a photo and held it up.

She nodded. "Yeah, he's one of our neighbors. Real friendly guy."

"Well, I caught him breaking into your apartment, trying to install bugging devices."

She felt that bit of steady foundation she'd been working hard to firm up under her feet had washed away again. She stared up at him in shock. "He was what?" she croaked. She reached for his cheek and whispered, "Are you serious?"

With his arm still around her more for emotional support than anything, he nodded. "We caught him. He's at the police station, and he's talking. He was hired by your kidnapper."

"Will the shocks ever stop?" She shook her head. "So, not only was this guy stalking me but he was using this guy as well?"

"Now, if only we could stop him from finding out that we'd caught Ross," Miles said, "but it's already too late for that."

"I don't understand," she said. But he'd already taken the crutches from her and tucked them inside the vehicle, then helped her into her seat. With her safely buckled in, he walked around to the front seat's passenger side, while Nico got into the driver's side. There, Miles twisted to look at her and explained everything that had gone on.

"But then this Ambrose guy knows that Ross will talk?"

"Exactly. Which means Ambrose has a backup plan," Nico said. "Otherwise he'd be worried and potentially would have taken Ross out rather than let him talk."

"Or the information that Ross has is really of no value," Miles iterated. "Any of those options are possible, but you can bet the police are all over Ambrose's third place as well as Ross's apartment."

"So we have an awful lot happening on the case," she said brightly, trying to see all the positive things going on. Because really, they had found the apartment across from the one where she had been kidnapped and held. And in her own apartment, they'd found a connection too, and, sure enough, it was a neighbor that she'd always thought was a bit flighty and young and just looking to score, but instead he was being paid to do all kinds of nasty things by this guy. "I wonder why Ross did that."

"Money," Miles said. "Apparently he's a bit of a hacker and still hasn't quite made the grade. Doesn't have a steady job and potentially is a music lover."

She nodded. "That's his other love. Playing music and computer games. He's pretty decent at his music from what I've heard from inside my place, but I don't think he's ever made it big anywhere."

"So he needed money. And this offered him pretty good pay for very little work."

"And he could have delivered that meal for me to my captor? Ross could have seen me tied up inside?"

"Ross is no saint, and, yes, he delivered meals to Ambrose. But Ross was not let inside these apartments as a rule, it seems. So Ross may not have seen you tied up. If we can believe Ross at all, he didn't know Ambrose was delivering women. Ross thought Ambrose was delivering *packages*."

She was amazed and saddened by everything she found out. "You think that you live in a normal world and that everybody around you is normal. Then you find out that they're all conspiring against you."

"Not quite," Miles said. "You can't judge everybody by

one or two bad apples."

"But you know that I will," she said firmly. "It doesn't matter if I really want to or not, but essentially I will because it'll be this experience that I draw on." His look was so understanding and compassionate that it almost brought tears to her eyes. Something she'd been desperately trying to hold back.

"I understand that," he said. "And again that's why you need some time to deal with this trauma on top of the previous trauma, so that they don't compound in your mind."

She gave a raw laugh at that as she stared out at the traffic going by and the people zooming by in a steady pace in the world outside, whereas it felt like everything inside her had come to a shatteringly screeching halt. She didn't even know what to say, so she said nothing and slumped in the corner of the vehicle.

When they pulled up to the front of her apartment, Miles got out and helped her onto the sidewalk, then grabbed her crutches and nodded to Nico, who drove away again. "Now where is he going?"

"To park the vehicle," he said. "There isn't any street parking here."

She nodded. "It's one of the reasons I like it," she said. "I didn't have to worry about vehicles parked all around the place. It would always be moving traffic." And, when they got to the front steps, she looked up and groaned. "This doesn't look like fun."

He chuckled and said, "Grab your crutches."

She looked at him in surprise and said, "I have my crutches." She took them from under her armpits held them together.

"Hold them," he said.

She instinctively grabbed them, and he bent and scooped her up into his arms and carried her up the steps. She looked at him in surprise. "It's very unusual to get carried when you're an adult," she said.

"Maybe, but I've had to do it many times."

"I'm pretty tall. Most men wouldn't even try."

"You're tall but lean and light as a feather," he said.

She snorted at that. "You should hear my photographer. She's always moaning and groaning that I should lose weight."

He set her down at the top of the steps with an astonished look. "Are you serious?"

She nodded. "I think it's the death of the actual modeling industry. You can never be a healthy weight for them. They always tell you that the cameras add ten pounds, and they can't afford that."

"Then they need to find better cameras," he said. "In this world, where we can put a person on the moon, why can't we find a camera that doesn't add ten pounds? How about a camera that takes away ten pounds? I'm sure that would be something that would sell like hotcakes."

She chuckled at that. They quickly maneuvered through the first set of double doors at the main entrance and into the hallway and then to her apartment. There she found a guard outside, the same one who she had seen inside the hospital. She stopped and stared at him, then said, "How did you get here before me?"

He grinned. "I walked."

"Oh. That explains it," She gave him a bright smile and entered her room. All her smiles fell away as she saw three techs inside her apartment, scanning things with devices in their hands, going over everything in her apartment. She turned to look at Miles.

"Just in case Ambrose or Ross were already here once before," he said in a low tone. "So don't talk if you don't have to."

She pinched her lips together and hobbled into the kitchen. There she stopped and looked around. The techs had placed a lot of the equipment they needed on the kitchen table, but the counter itself was clear. She couldn't remember the last time she'd shopped or if her sister had, but the one thing Vanessa really wanted right now was coffee.

Miles seemed to anticipate her needs though, as he moved the coffeemaker forward so he could fill the back canister with water and then hunted in the cupboards for coffee grounds.

"I have beans and a grinder," she offered.

"Point me where," he said and proceeded to follow her instructions to make the coffee for her pot.

With that dripping, she headed slowly to her bedroom. She was grateful that she found no techs working here. She looked back at him and whispered, "Is it safe in here?"

He shrugged. "I'll find out."

As she made her way to the bed, he disappeared behind her.

But he was back in a few minutes and nodded. "They've already checked this room," he said.

"Good. And it's clear?" She knew he had just said that, but, for whatever reason, she really wanted to have it as coldly clear-cut as she could make it.

"Yes, your bedroom is clear."

She nodded and slowly sank down on the bed. "Now the doc said I could go home and take it easy," she said. "He didn't say I couldn't have a shower though, did he?"

"Are you sure you're ready for that?"

She shot him a look. "The question is, can I tolerate being in my skin one more day without it?"

"Ah," he said. He stood beside her for a moment and nodded. "How about a bath instead?"

She looked up at him, puzzled. "What's the difference?"

"A bath means you won't have to stand on that bad ankle. You'll sit and wash your hair, and you'll soak away the feeling of somebody else's hands on you."

She winced. "I forgot about my ankle," she said, kicking her legs up so they were both elevated. "It's not that bad."

"You don't want a bath?"

"I want a bath too much," she admitted. "But a lot of strangers are here. With a shower, I could get in and get out faster and be clean. But a bath? I'd want to soak and relax and feel like I was home alone. But, with all the strangers around, it doesn't feel that way."

"Well, it could be if we wait a few moments."

"Will they be done that fast?" she asked. She shifted back on the bed and stretched out full-length. "If that's the case, I could wait."

"How long can you wait?" he asked as he walked to the door. "I can ask them."

"Please do," she murmured. She watched as he stepped out of the bedroom and closed the door gently behind him. She was almost surprised he did that. It was the first time she'd been in a room alone, except for the hospital bathroom, since she'd escaped. It felt both good and bad, as if the umbilical cord between her and Miles had stretched enough to allow him to do that.

Of course he hadn't been there in the hospital the entire

time. She'd been there, but Miles had left Nico, another equally dependable and strong alpha male to look after her. So she hadn't necessarily felt the loss of Miles's presence quite so badly. She was more than a little worried about what would happen when these two men had to leave her though, as she'd become accustomed to having them here. And it had only been twenty-four hours. Like, what did that make her? Besides a pitifully weak woman? That's the one thing she refused to be though.

She swung her legs around again and forced herself to sit up, wincing at the pain in her ribs. But he was right. It would be much easier on her body if she sat in the bathtub. The shower would be faster and maybe less vulnerable to stand there. But the bath would feel much better.

When he returned a moment later, he nodded and said, "They're almost done. Give them five."

She smiled. "In that case, I'll lie here and rest until they're gone. Come back and tell me when they are, please."

"Will do," he said cheerfully, and he walked back out again, closing the door behind him again. She eased back down on the bed and groaned. She was just tired enough now that she was here and home that maybe she would sleep. If she went into a hot, soaking bath, she would probably be so tired from the heat and the comfort that, when she came out, she'd probably nap again. And maybe that was okay too. She closed her eyes and rested. But it wasn't even ten minutes later when he rapped on the door and stepped inside.

"Okay, they're gone."

She smiled. "So, it's just the three of us here?"

"Two of us," he said. "Nico has gone out to do some more reconnaissance work."

"There's nothing to be done," she said, "until somebody spots that asshole."

"Not true," he said. "This guy's got money. He's rented or bought several apartments, and we're tracking down other names to see if he might have other money and other apartments elsewhere."

"I guess you have to give an ID to buy or rent a place, don't you?"

He nodded. "And IDs aren't terribly cheap. He may have one or two, or possibly three or four, but that doesn't mean he has more than that."

"Plus you have to keep track of them and carry all that information with you," she said. "So I would say two or three would make sense. But didn't you say he was also wanted in Europe? What IDs did he use there?"

"They have his legal name and four aliases all on file. Which would be triggered here if he used any of them. He's also known to have a maritime ship's wheel tattoo."

"Good. That's the guy that kidnapped me. And it would only be triggered if it was something that would alert the authorities," she said. "To rent an apartment, not so much. Especially if he was paying cash. He wouldn't need much in a way of a name at all."

"Right. However, now is a good time for a bath. Do you want me to run the water for you?"

"You can start it," she said as she slowly sat up again. "I almost fell asleep on the bed."

He looked back at her as he stepped into the bathroom. "Do you want a nap first?"

"No," she said. "I figured, when I come back out, I'd have a nap then. Warm baths tend to make me sleepy."

"And, if you can soak some of those sore muscles, you

might feel better faster," he said. "Do you have any bath salts?"

"I don't think so," she said. "I'll be fine without." She got up and hobbled her way to the bathroom, then pointed out a bottle of bubble bath and asked, "Can you add some of that please?"

And he poured in a good measure, and the two of them watched as the bubbles popped up immediately.

She sighed. "You know something? This was a really good idea."

"Good," he said. "Now, are you okay to get undressed and stripped down by yourself?"

She nodded. "Yes, I can do that. I got dressed on my own this morning."

"Good," he said. "It did cross my mind if you got Nico to help you."

She chuckled. "Not that it would bother you or anything."

"Well, it is one of the reasons why I was thinking maybe I should have been there. I did try to be there. But I'm glad you got dressed on your own."

She smiled at him. "Not to worry," she said. "I definitely don't have the same reaction to him as I do to you."

"Good," he said with a self-satisfied smile. "I'm glad to hear that."

"Well, that's nice," she said. "It's nice to know I made an impression anyway, even if it isn't the kind I wanted."

"You made the only kind that counts," he said quietly as he backed out of the small bathroom, his chest brushing ever-so-lightly against hers. "The kind that hit me in the heart." His words were meltingly soft and heartwarmingly honest.

"I'm glad. I was afraid that whatever was going on between us was just on my side."

"And I was afraid," he said, reaching up and tapping her lightly on the nose, "that whatever was going on was because you were grateful and needed to feel safe."

"I've been worried about that too," she said. "Except for the fact that, every time I get an option, I turned to you and nobody else."

"Could be the same thing," he said, raising an eyebrow.

She smiled, turned away and said, "You'll see. I don't know why, and I don't know how. I'm not sure that we'll even do anything about it, but definitely something is between us."

"Agreed," he said. "Have a bath. I'll go set up and do some work." As he went to step out and close the door, he said, "Don't fall asleep, please."

"In the bath, you mean?"

He nodded.

"Why not?" she asked, puzzled. "There's not really any reason not to, is there?"

"Well, I'll have to check on you a couple times, and I really don't want to interrupt you if you're sleeping, but I wouldn't want you to sleep in here either. Because you can't answer me when I call out to you."

"Well, I'll do my best not to fall asleep," she said. "How's that?"

"Good enough," he said. "And if you need help getting out because of that ankle, let me know."

"That would be dangerous," she muttered under her breath.

But he heard her and chuckled. "But I live a dangerous life, remember?"

He headed back out to the living room and sat down with his laptop. All the lights were off, and the curtains were closed, as if to make it seem like nobody was home. He didn't know if their kidnapper Ambrose/Stahl would put in a listening device himself or if he figured now that they had Ross picked up that the local cops would check for things like that. Still, Miles wanted to be ready.

This guy was very good at what he did, but this was a new game for him now that the police had his name and several aliases, three of his apartments and Ross. So whether Ambrose liked the game or was irritated by it or was unnerved by the changes, Miles didn't know. He hoped for the latter because unnerved would mean that Ambrose could make mistakes. And this guy needed to make a mistake because, unfortunately so far, nobody had found out enough about him.

With his laptop, Miles worked on all the information they had so far. Scotland Yard and MI6 and Interpol and also his Mavericks team had searches going on for every name they'd had on Ambrose to date. Miles set up a new search for leaseholds and vehicles and another for phone companies and internet service.

Ambrose had to have cell phones of some kind. It's possible he used burner phones and threw them away every time, but it's also possible that one of his aliases had a dedicated phone. With all of that running in the background, he got up and poured himself the first cup of coffee out of the pot. Then, realizing she hadn't even gotten one, he wondered if he should take her one. But she was in the bath. Knowing it was a little more dangerous, but still the right thing to do, he walked into the bedroom and called out through the bathroom door. "You didn't get coffee," he said.

"Damn," she muttered. "I didn't, did I?"

"Are you decently covered in bubbles?" he asked. "I'll go pour you a cup."

"Actually," she said, "I am."

"Okay, back in a minute." He went to the kitchen and poured her a cup. Then he frowned as he hadn't asked if she took anything in it, but he cast his mind back to the hospital and realized she hadn't complained either way. With the cup in his hand, he walked back to the bathroom and gently undid the door so that he didn't spill anything. Then he stepped in, keeping his eyes on the cup.

He set the cup on the side of the bathtub, and she whispered, "Won't you even look at me?"

He shook his head. "May be better if I didn't," he said, taking several steps backward. And then he grinned and said, "But, hey, who could resist?" And he took one long look at the absolutely beautiful woman, her feet tucked atop the tub at the end, ankles crossed, with her bruised one on top. And he could see brightly painted toenails that he had somehow missed up till now. There were little chipped signs of her rough few days, and the rest of her was covered in light and fluffy bubbles right up to her chin. He grinned. "Gorgeous. But, yeah, you didn't need me to tell you that."

"No, but it's nice to hear anyway," she said. "And, while you're here, can you pass me the shampoo?" And she pointed to the top of the counter.

He reached for the bottle she requested and brought it over, then set it down on the side and said, "Call out if you need me. And watch out for that shampoo with your stitches."

Then he disappeared. Back in the bedroom, he grinned like a fool. It was foolish to get involved with anybody in the case like this, but it was pretty damn hard not to, considering who she was and who he was. He wasn't known for playing around and certainly not when on a mission. But everything seemed different this time around, or maybe it was just because he wanted it to be different because he wanted to have a reason to spend time with her.

When his phone rang, it was Nico.

"Is she doing okay now?

"She's soaking in a bath," he said, his tone neutral. "She wanted to get the feel of that man off her."

"But she wasn't raped?" Nico asked.

"Not as far as I know," Miles said.

"Good," Nico said. "After everything she's been through, that's almost a given. But, if he was saving her for somebody else, then that's understandable."

"Yes. Have you gotten anywhere?"

"No, I've been flashing his face and the sketch all over the car rental companies, leasing companies, anything to do with telecommunications. Even the electronics companies. But so far, nobody's seen anything. Very convenient, right?"

"I know," Miles said. "The trouble is, Ambrose could have used a proxy to check out these rentals, before he showed up to do the actual paperwork. Plus a ton of people live here, just in these first couple blocks. I wonder if we can access more people via email."

"Well, if you want to start contacting some of the bigger cell phone providers or leasing agents," he said, "we could potentially send them the sketch or the Interpol photo. Maybe both and see if anybody recognizes him."

"I'll do that now," he said. "When you come back, do

you want to bring some food?"

"Will do," Nico said, and he hung up.

Miles grabbed his phone and contacted several of the bigger stores around town that had branches all over the city and farther out. Once he got through to the managers and explained who he was and what he was doing, he got permission to email the photos and asked them to speak to their employees. He knew it was fishing with a wide net and potentially nothing would be gained, but they had to do something.

Otherwise this guy was living as a ghost completely off the grid. The car rental places were a good place to check and so were gas stations. But, if he himself wasn't driving, which was quite possible after seeing him at Ross's capture, then Ross was still their best lead.

At that, he froze and quickly called Nico back. "Are you coming home now?"

"I'll be there in about ten. I just stopped and picked up food. Why?"

"I want to see Ross's apartment. I can't believe we didn't even think of that."

"Didn't the cops?"

"I don't think so. We had a mess with the other forensics at the third apartment, with all its booby traps."

"I'll be there soon. Hang on," Nico said.

Miles got up and refilled his coffee, then realized this pot was pretty much gone so tossed back the last little bit of it and shut off the coffeemaker. Nico came in a few minutes later. Miles walked back into the bedroom and said, "Hey, Nico just came with food. Do you want anything?"

"What, will you deliver food to the bathtub too?" she said with a laugh.

"I could if you want me to." He turned to see Nico with his head poked into the bedroom and watching as Miles talked through the bathroom door. "But, if you think you'll be out soon, we'll wait for you."

"I'm done in here," she said. "I just rinsed off."

"Good," he said. "Then we'll set it up and wait for you."

"Give me ten."

He headed back to the kitchen, closing the master bedroom door as he went.

"Did I just hear your sweetie?" Nico asked with a straight face.

Miles shrugged. He wouldn't get into a discussion about Vanessa and him if he could avoid it. The trouble was, Nico knew him from the old days and avoiding talk about Vanessa would be almost impossible.

"I guess it's really different now, isn't it?" Nico asked in a contemplative voice, surprising Miles.

"What's different?"

"How different the missions are, and, although relationships happen, you were always one to hold back."

"I know," he said. "I've been contemplating that now too."

"Nothing is stopping you," he said. "She's not involved. She's been a victim. That's the only thing though. Just make sure there's no odd imbalance of emotions here."

"I've already thought of that," he said. He smiled at his friend, recognizing the concern in his voice. "I'll be fine. Don't worry about it."

"You might be fine," Nico said, "but I'll worry no matter what." He grinned. "That's what friends are for."

"Good enough," Miles said in a mild tone. "But you've been warned."

Nico chuckled. They quickly brought out the food that he had picked up, which appeared to be a selection of beef pies and fries and just more carbs.

"You know she's a model and probably won't eat most of this, right?"

"Didn't you say she ate two beef pies yesterday at the hospital?"

"I did," Miles nodded, understanding where Nico got that concept from. "But, at the same time, I'm pretty sure she's more into greens."

"Well, I have a Greek salad in the other bag," he said. "And a big one because I really wanted a salad too."

All of the food was now out on the table, and the two men sat down and discussed the search results to date.

"That's the problem," Nico said when Miles asked him. "So far, everything's turning up blank."

"And facial recognition hasn't come back yet either," Miles said. "But I would have presumed that, if they'd found something, they'd get a hold of us."

Just then his phone rang. He pulled it out to see one of the big electronics companies. "Hello. Miles here."

"One of our staff thinks she may have seen this man," said the manager on the other end.

"Do we know when?"

"She thought it was two days ago. I'm bringing up the video feed at the store," he said.

"Perfect," Miles said. "If you can capture him on the feed, that would be huge. At least we could track his movements in your store at a specific time."

"Ah, there he is," the man said. "I presume you'll need to collect this?"

"Yes. I'll send somebody around for it. Do you have a

list of what he's buying?"

"Several phones," he said. "And it looks like a set of rabbit ears for internet use while driving in a vehicle. Or at least that's how most of the people I know use them."

"Ah," Miles said. "Now that would make sense. Okay. We'll send somebody from the local police department around to collect that if you could have it ready, please."

"No problem," he said and hung up.

Miles sat back and explained to Nico what the guy had found.

Nico laughed. "That's old school, but it works if people haven't secured their networks."

"But a lot of networks are wide open," Miles said, "so he could sit in his vehicle and have internet access from anybody close by. He doesn't need his own provider."

"True, but I wonder how long before that gets to be enough."

"But we're back to having a home base somewhere."

"Did we ever check the Interpol information for girlfriends or a girlfriend's siblings?"

"No, that's an interesting idea," Miles said as he got up. He snagged his laptop and brought up the information. He quickly went through it. "There was a girlfriend, but that was a lot of years ago."

"How many years?"

He frowned and nodded. "Seventeen."

"Interesting." Nico got up and came around to look at the name. "Let's add that name to all the searches. It's genderless enough that it could be male or female."

But, as soon as he typed it in, up came an obituary. "She's dead," he said. He searched further and found a police file. "It's so weird when we have access to all the databases, and the Mavericks search function just seems to run through them all."

"But I like it," Nico said. "At least we're getting information firsthand instead of waiting and waiting."

"Like we are for the facial recognition from the Realtors?"

"That's more or less because we can't do it all ourselves. Oh, but I did find the guy's name on that lease that got rejected on the apartment where Ambrose held Vanessa."

"And?" Miles prodded.

"John Lennon."

Miles shook his head. "Not surprising. Confirmed my earlier theory."

Nico found a photo for the girlfriend, looked at the woman's face and said, "Interesting. Look at this."

"What's that?"

"A redhead."

They both stared at the woman and her bright orangey-red hair and her silken white skin.

Nico asked, "Remind you of anybody?"

"Yeah, especially over the passage of time," he said.

"But we already knew this was our guy," Nico stated.

"No," Miles said. "We didn't know that our guy was picking women from his own life. We were assuming that he was picking them and giving them to somebody else."

"Right," Nico said, frowning at that fine distinction. "So, did he hate her then? Is he picking up women that he wants to suffer and then selling them off?"

"That's an interesting idea," Miles said. "Hard to say though. But we can add that to our list of hypotheses." He brought up his notes and quickly added in the girlfriend's name while her death was added to the files. Then he said,

"Oh, this is interesting."

"You're saying that a lot lately," Nico said. "What do you have now?"

"She was beaten to death."

"By our suspect?"

"Nobody was ever caught for it. He was locked up as a suspect at the time but released."

"Then it could be where he started?"

"Maybe," Miles said, "but I'm wondering how much we really don't know about this case. It seems like every time we come up to one layer, more layers are underneath."

"But other than that, what other reason could there be?"

Miles shook his head. "I don't even want to hazard a guess."

"I do," Vanessa said from behind him. "Several in fact. He might have hated her because she had an affair, and he beat her to death. He might have loved her, and she spurned his advances, so he beat her to death. Or he had nothing to do with her death, and it was her death that spurred him to kill off more like her."

"But why would anybody who loved her want to kill everybody else that was in her image?" Miles asked.

"It could be because they *were* in her image, and they shouldn't be alive if she wasn't. Maybe he saw them as pale copies," she said as she stared at the photo in amazement. "That's seriously a close likeness to me, isn't it?"

"But you're sure he said that another man was coming to check you out?"

She nodded, but her gaze didn't leave the photo. "That's what he said."

"Any reason to believe he was lying?"

"I don't know," she said. "But is there any reason to believe him either? Like I said, maybe he's doing this to punish her. Maybe for dying?" When the men stared at her in surprise, she shrugged. "Who knows what's in the mind of somebody like this?"

"True enough." Miles got up and pulled out a chair for her. "Get off that leg," he scolded lightly.

She rolled her eyes at him. "Who knew you were such a nursemaid?"

At Nico's chuckle, she turned to him and said, "I doubt you'd be any different." But she sat down and surveyed the food. "This looks like guy food."

"And I thought of you too," Nico said, motioning toward the big Greek salad.

Her eyes lit up. "Okay, now you're forgiven." She served herself a large bowl of salad and took the smallest of the pies.

The men tucked into the rest of it.

"What do you mean by punish her?"

"Just because somebody dies doesn't mean that the people left behind are ready to let them go," she said. "I mean, obviously we are only making conjectures as to who and what he is, but there could be a lot of reasons. And maybe he hated her. Maybe his love turned to hate because his world shifted at that point. And maybe what had been all bright and sunny had turned dark and ugly after her death. And now he's killing her over and over again."

"Or making her suffer the way he suffered?" Miles added.

"That's quite true," she said. "But, until we have a chance to ask the psychopath, we won't know."

"And we're assuming that he was serious about another man coming," Nico said.

"Right," Miles answered, "so we should find out who

that man is, and there has to be some communication between them."

"And how do we find him?" Nico asked, turning to Vanessa. "Did Ambrose give you any idea where the buyer was coming from or how far away he was traveling? Anything?"

She shook her head. "Not that I remember. There wasn't anything in the apartments?"

"Not the one where he held you. That place was pretty cleared out by the time the police got inside. But I do have photos that were left on a table in the apartment across the hall, his temporary home away from home," he said, bringing them up so she could see them.

She winced when she glanced down. As they went through several, she said, "That's my house. That's on the way to work. That's just outside my apartment." Then she shook her head. "I don't see anything in these that indicates another man."

"No," Miles added. "I don't either."

"What about the airports?" she asked.

"Sure," Nico said, "but you know how many men come through the country every day? And, of course, the buyer could have come on the ferry, or he could have had his own boat, and he could have been just on the mainland coming in from the outside of town."

"Right, and he didn't try to pretty you up or do anything like that?" Miles asked.

She shook her head. "No, I don't think he was invested in how I looked, outside of the fact that I was *the* look."

"Interesting," Miles said yet again. "So he wasn't worried about your value going up or down depending on how you looked."

"No, I don't think so," she said as she took several bites of the Greek salad.

"Well, there will be a reason," Nico said. "We just haven't figured it out yet."

"No, not yet," she said.

Just then Miles got a phone call. He picked it up to find it was Ryker.

"We have a citizen contacting the police, saying that a man kidnapped a redhead right off the street."

"A redhead?" He turned to look at Vanessa. "Where?"

"That's why I'm calling. It's literally between the two apartments, Vanessa's home and where she was held captive. At that one corner. If you go out the front door to the left, it's almost at the end of that corner."

"Did the traffic cameras pick it up?"

"Yes, it's him, although we aren't getting a clear shot of his face, but unfortunately it looks like it's Vanessa's sister."

"And where did he go with her?"

"He appears to have gotten into a vehicle. We have the license plate, and we've tracked it around the corner and another corner again."

"Please tell me that you didn't lose it?"

"We haven't lost it, but it's parked and sitting at a coffee shop behind the building."

"How far away?"

"Not far." He gave Miles the address for Ambrose's third apartment.

"But he knows we know about his third apartment. He probably shot that detective inside his apartment himself."

"So it's a trap. I'm hoping that's the case," Ryker said. "You need to get over there fast."

Immediately Miles hung up the phone, then stood and

briefly explained to Vanessa what had happened. Hearing the eerie silence beside him, he turned.

She had a wide-eyed and horrified look on her face. "Was it Ruby?"

"We're not sure, but it's possible," he said.

She looked over at Nico. "Please go with Miles and save my sister."

Nico nodded. "The guard outside will stay with you."

She stared at him. "I don't want him to stay. If Ambrose has Ruby, let me come."

"And what good will that do?" Miles asked, but he already knew the answer.

"He can take me again in exchange for my sister."

"That's not happening," Miles said. "He won't get to either of you."

"Wrong," she whispered sadly, shrinking in on herself with her arms wrapped tight around her knees and rocking back and forth. "He's already got her." He hated to leave, but he had to. He bent down and gave her a hard kiss. "Stay safe and stay inside, please." And he turned and walked out with Nico.

As soon as Miles was outside, he told the guard to get inside and to not let anybody else in unless it was him or Nico. "And I don't care if it's the high commissioner. Nobody comes in, got it?"

The guard nodded. "Got it."

And they took off toward the third known apartment. They went out the back way across the large green space where Ruby liked to sit and headed into the other building.

CHAPTER 12

VANESSA LOOKED UP at the guard with watery eyes and said, "Sorry you're on babysitting duty again. I hope you don't mind."

"It's all good," he said comfortably. "Hey, look at that food."

"If you missed lunch, feel free," she said. "My appetite's definitely gone." Then she got up. "I gotta put on coffee. Will you have a cup?"

"Sure," he said.

She walked over to the coffeemaker and put out another small pot. As she smiled at the guard, she said, "I really appreciate you looking after me."

"Hey, it's not a hardship," he said. "It's what I do."

"Are you a guard all the time?"

He shook his head. "No, just most of the time."

"Okay," she said. "Well, those of us who need it appreciate it." She sat down and forced herself to take a little bit more of the salad. But that's about all she could do. She wasn't even dressed yet. "While the coffee drips, I'll get dressed, and then I'll come back and eat some more." With a smile, she disappeared into her room.

Then she quickly dressed and returned to the kitchen, but there was no sign of the guard. She froze and looked around the living room and then realized he had to be in the bathroom. As she headed toward the bathroom, it was empty. Under her breath, she whispered, "Oh, God. Oh, God. Oh, God." She hadn't even gotten the guy's name, had she? She racked her brain, thought he was called Sammy. "Sammy, where are you?"

But there was no answer. His plate was half empty, as if he'd stopped midbite. And she realized he'd probably been called to help Nico and Miles at the other apartment. She walked out onto the small balcony and stared across the green space. She was hoping she would see Sammy racing over there to help the other two men but saw nothing. He'd left her alone, so there had to be a damn good reason. As she headed to the front door though, she realized it wasn't even locked.

Immediately she threw the bolts on and turned around with her back to the door, eyes closed and whispering, "Please, please, somebody come back." But there was no answer to her soft call, and there was no sign of Sammy anywhere. It's the only thing that made sense though. She hadn't checked to see if maybe somebody from the hospital had gotten mad that he was here and maybe he'd been phoned and told to get back to work at the hospital. She quickly swiped the bolts and opened the door with a bright smile, expecting to see him standing there. But he wasn't.

She groaned and stepped back inside, then shut the door and relocked it. With her back against the door, she slowly slid to the floor. "Now what the hell is going on?" She pulled out her phone and sent a message to Miles. **I don't know where you are,** she typed, **but the security guard disappeared.**

She waited for an answer and realized there was none. And he had probably put his phone on Silent so as not to disturb whoever was hiding out at the other apartment. Caught between a rock and a hard place, she sat here motionless for a few minutes, sending a text to the local detective on this case, while hoping that her sister was safe. She didn't know who to even call next, but, as long as she sat here and didn't bring back any of the people who were helping her sister, that's what was really important. She was safe. Somebody had to help Ruby.

As she sat here though, she thought she heard a sound outside. She got up and looked out the window to see a fight going on outside the main front entrance. She studied the men but didn't recognize any of them, and none of them were Sammy. But she couldn't take her eyes off of it. Finally it seemed like the disturbance calmed down, and the men went on their way. And, if nothing else, it had taken her mind off everything else for a few moments. Now though, she returned to worrying, her panic worse than ever.

She headed to her bedroom, chilled even though it was a warm day, and reached for a sweater that she had flung on the back of her chair. It almost always lived there. She was pretty good about putting away most of her clothes, but this sweater was the coziest one that was way too big and came down way too long. It was stretched and outsized and faded in color and full of little hairy bits all over, and she absolutely loved it. She refused to get rid of it at any time.

As she headed back toward the kitchen, intent on pouring herself a cup of coffee, she heard another sound. She immediately bolted toward the front window and then stopped and realized the sound had come from behind her, like a door closing. She headed back to the bedroom ever-so-slowly but found nothing there. But the closet doors were open. The front hall closet was closed though, and beside it was a big double-doored closet, where the washing machine and dryer were. Slowly she opened it. And nothing was there.

As she turned and walked away, a man called out, "Boo." His arm snaked around her neck and tugged her up tight against a hard chest. She fought like crazy, but she could barely even breathe. And then a hard voice spoke in her ear and whispered, "Boo-hoo. You're caught again. Now you're mine."

And before she lost consciousness in his chokehold, she realized her captor … was Sammy.

MILES AND NICO were on either side of Ambrose's third apartment door, and, so far, they hadn't seen anybody. Just as they thought they heard a sound, Miles leaned forward and turned the knob and pushed it open. The two of them lunged into this apartment, one going high and one going low, and searched. The techs had finished working on this crime scene, but this apartment was empty. Miles and Nico quickly searched the front rooms and headed to the bedroom. They found Ruby tied up on the bed in the same way as her sister had been. He raced over and quickly cut the binds holding her, then rolled her over gently. "Ruby? Wake up."

Her eyelids fluttered open. She stared up at him in surprise. And then she seemed to realize what had happened, and she bolted upright. "Go, go, go," she said. "You have to go back." He stared at her in shock. "I was a diversion," she screamed. "Go back! My sister. They're after my sister!"

Nico stared, but Miles was already in motion. His heart

pounded fast against his ribs as he bolted back the way they'd come. It had never even occurred to him that it was a ruse to get him away from Vanessa. He knew he should have listened to his gut and not left her alone, but she'd insisted on them doing anything for her sister. But he had left Vanessa alone with Sammy. Damn it. There was a good chance that poor guard was dead too now.

As he turned around the corner, he saw Nico and Ruby racing behind him. He came bolting around the corner and headed up to the front door, taking the steps two at a time. Then he crashed through the double front doors. There was no sign of Sammy, but then he should have been inside her apartment anyway. He pushed Vanessa's apartment door open, stepped inside and froze. An empty hollowness greeted him. And he knew—he knew inside—that whoever it was had already grabbed her. There was a note on the floor, just a piece of scrap paper, that floated down to lay on top of the carpet. He picked it up very carefully on one corner and read the note as Nico and Ruby came running inside.

Too late.

Miles could almost hear the silent laughter running through the apartment. He didn't dare believe the note, but, as Nico and Ruby raced through the place, screaming and yelling for Vanessa, Miles knew that they were already too late. He stood outside onto the front steps, studying the traffic and the traffic lights and the traffic cams. "Maybe without Ross …" He had his phone and Ryker on the other end already. "It was a trick," he snapped. "They took Vanessa."

"Shit. We're on the traffic cameras."

"Nothing is happening out front."

"He took her out back."

Miles raced back inside her apartment. "Send me the feed," he said. He opened up his laptop and grabbed the link off the chat, then brought up the feed as Vanessa was carried, seemingly unconscious, out the back door. But it was the man carrying her that made his heart freeze. "God damn it," he said. "The man carrying her is Sammy, the guard."

"What?" Nico came racing and took a look behind his shoulder. "Damn. How did he do that?"

"I don't know if that's the buyer who was after her or if that's the man that we're looking for," Miles whispered under his breath. "Or whether they just got to Sammy somehow." He was busy following feeds to see that they got into a vehicle, and the license plate had been removed, but it was enough that he could see the make and model of the car. And, with Nico checking, they realized Sammy had a vehicle just like that one registered to himself.

"So, he's using his own vehicle. I'll suggest that he was paid a hell of a lot of money to do this then."

"We need to be on the road after her," Miles said, picking up his gear. He tossed a look at Nico. "You drive. I'll follow the feeds." They were in their vehicle within thirty seconds, refusing to take Ruby, but had waited long enough for her to make calls to get picked up. When two officers snagged her up and promised to take her to the hospital, then Nico and Miles were already on the road and out after Vanessa. The traffic cams sent a thousand feeds all the time as they searched left, right, at every intersection, following Sammy's car slowly through them all.

Finally the vehicle pulled into an underground parking lot. They were less than two minutes behind, and that's when they lost track of him. Miles immediately ordered names and contact information from Ryker for every apartment in the building.

"Sammy lives there," Ryker said. "This makes no sense. Stay on the line, Miles."

They drove into the car park and pulled up behind the vehicle in question, then called for backup and waited for the cops to come and grab the vehicle, knowing that no way would she be in it. They did a quick check anyway.

"What apartment number?" Miles asked.

"Third floor," Ryker said. "Three zero eight."

They took the stairs, racing up, weapons already in their hands. By the time they made it up to the third floor, the two of them looked at each other. "You know this makes no sense, right?" Nico asked Miles.

"I know," Miles said. "I'm afraid somebody else has a vehicle down there, and, now that we're up here, they're taking off." And he quickly relayed that message to Ryker.

"We're watching the feeds for vehicles coming out of the underground car park," he said. "You check the apartment. We're on the parking lot angle."

Miles gave the count of three, and they literally busted through the door in to Sammy's apartment. And they found Sammy, all right. A Sammy. Possibly the rightful owner of this apartment. But he was dead. And he certainly wasn't the Sammy who had been standing guard at the hospital, but there was an uncanny resemblance. Nico and Miles looked at each other in horror, spun and called it.

Even as Miles talked to Ryker, he raced back downstairs for the vehicle. "What vehicle has left in the last ten minutes?" he asked.

"A small white pickup. I've got the license plate. We're tracking it right now."

"We need several units here. The real Sammy's dead.

And it's not the same man who was the fake security guard at the hospital or at Vanessa's apartment."

"Shit," he said. "Any chance you have a photo of him?"

"I do," Miles said. "I took it when he first arrived." While Nico drove, Miles quickly searched through his photos and sent it to Ryker. "Let me know if you can find him."

"Oh, I found him," Ryker said. "He's actually criminally related to our buddy Ambrose here. He's wanted all over the eastern block of Europe."

"Any idea where he's going right now?"

"Out of town and most likely to a private boat. We need to get him fast."

"Set up roadblocks," Miles said immediately. "We'll have to cut off as many of his exits as we can."

"We're on it," Ryker said.

In the background, Miles could hear Ryker's fingers clicking away. "We need to contact Interpol." He looked over to see Nico already talking to somebody, presumably his cohorts at MI5. "I wonder if this is the buyer who was to pick her up?"

"It's possible," Ryker said. "I don't know."

"It doesn't matter," Miles said. "We have to get her back."

And then the chase was on. Nico came around several corners and pointed. The pickup truck was pulling out of a gas station. And it was the one they wanted. The driver of the vehicle had seen them coming up from behind and hit the gas.

Miles told Ryker to track him. "We're following him now," he said. "We're heading north. Let's cut him off with a roadblock as soon as we can. He can't be allowed to get free this time."

"Any sign of her?"

"No," he said. "That's the one thing that really bothers me. What if she's not even in there?"

"She's probably unconscious, so either slumped over in the front," Nico said, "or he's got her jammed in the small seat in the back."

"Maybe." He quickly told Ryker to get the feed from the gas station.

When that came up, he checked and said, "She's there, but she's slumped against the passenger's door."

"Good. He's getting sloppy."

"This was an improvised plan," Ryker said. "And, without the planning that they normally go through, so I'll say this one'll be the one that trips them up."

But the pickup was pulling faster away from them. Miles looked over at Nico. "No more gas to give this SUV?"

"I don't know," he said. "Whatever engine he's got in there has been souped-up. He's got way more speed than I've got."

The chat window popped up on the laptop in front of him. **Roadblock two miles ahead.**

"Just keep him in sight," Miles told Nico. "A roadblock's two miles up."

Nico nodded. The truck inched ahead ever-so-slightly, putting more distance between them, but such a long stretch of road was here that he could keep him in sight. And then, when the police roadblock came into sight at a bend in the road up ahead, the truck hit the brakes and spun around and pulled a U-turn, and then he seemed to change his mind and went slashing through a rough field on the side instead, taking out a fence post.

Shots were fired all over the truck, coming from the police roadblock.

"Jesus Christ, they'll kill her," Miles cried out.

The shooting did not stop the fake Sammy. Nico went tearing through the field, gaining on them. Miles opened up his side window and pulled out his handgun, then leveled a shot and took out a back tire. The truck fishtailed terribly. He lined up again and shot at the back window, near fake Sammy's head.

"You want to remember that, at this speed," Nico said, "if you take out the driver, that vehicle might flip over and kill her."

Miles swore under his breath because he knew that too. But the truck was having trouble maintaining its path as it was. Miles heard sirens behind him as the other police vehicles behind them caught up. "Any chance of coming up on the inside of him and forcing him off into those rocks? He'll have a hard time getting away, driving in this rough field."

Nico nodded, and, as they neared the pickup, the fake Sammy sent a shot through the passenger window, breaking the SUV's windshield but missing Nico and Miles.

"Great," Miles said.

But it was obvious that the truck was struggling to stay ahead of them with the one shot out tire.

Miles lined up and took out a front tire. The truck immediately skidded sideways in the field, unable to stay on course, rolling to a slow stop.

Miles was already out of his vehicle, running, holding a gun up against the driver well before Nico ever came to a stop right in front of the pickup. The other cops raced up to joined them too.

Miles jerked open the driver's side door and placed a handgun against the temple of the driver. "Nice try, *Sammy*," he snapped. He jerked the man out and dropped him to the ground, digging his knee into the fake Sammy's back. Two cops came over immediately, and he let them secure the prisoner while he dove into the front seat, his fingers going to Vanessa's neck and checking for a pulse. She was alive. But there was fresh blood. He raced around to the far side, opened up the passenger-side door, and yelled, "We need an ambulance."

"Has she been shot?" Nico asked.

"Yes. I don't think it's too serious," he said. "But it looks like her shoulder was hit." He quickly held a hand over the wound that was slowly and slightly pulsing blood. As he undid the buckle of the seat belt around her, he whispered, "Vanessa, please, please, sweetie, wake up."

Finally her eyes fluttered open, and she stared up at him. As soon as she recognized him, tears filled her eyes, and she whispered, "I told you that you shouldn't leave me."

"Yes," he said in a dry tone. "You also told me, rather adamantly, if you will remember, that I was supposed to save your sister."

Her eyes widened at that. "Did you?"

He nodded. "Ruby's safe."

She smiled and slid her good arm up around his neck. "Then it's all worthwhile."

"I don't know about that," he said. "It looks like a bullet nicked your shoulder."

"Is it major?"

He studied the wound, then shook his head. "Looks like a flesh wound."

"Then who cares?" she whispered as she tucked up close

against his neck. "Promise you won't leave me." She held her gaze on him and repeated herself. "Promise you won't leave me."

"So you want me to stay long-term, forever even?" he asked, wondering.

"Could you? Would you?" She watched him closely as she asked.

"I would like that. And I wish I could promise you that, but I'll have to leave you some of the time, but just for my job."

She shuddered in his arms, and he just held her close.

"I guess that's fair," she said. "As long as we catch these guys, I'll be fine."

"I know you'll be fine," he whispered, "because you're an incredibly amazing woman." He paused, then added. "And I know you'll be fine because I'll be around as much as possible."

She tilted her head back, smiled up at him and said, "Now, if only we were alone and you were saying that …"

"Let's get that shoulder looked after," he said. "And then we'll see what we can do."

"Did you find the Ambrose guy?"

He shook his head. "Not yet."

She frowned. "Sammy said something about the other guy."

"What did he say?"

"Something about how his day was done, and I wouldn't have to worry about him anymore."

"Interesting," he said. "Well, we have his laptop here and his briefcase. It wouldn't break my heart at all if this guy shot his colleague Ambrose before kidnapping you."

"But if he killed him, we'll never really know why this

happened."

"Not quite true," Miles said, "because we still have your driver, *Sammy* here, and he's the asshole we need."

Just then another shot was fired, and he looked over to see the fake Sammy on the ground with one of the cops holding a handgun on him. And blood welled out of Sammy's shoulder.

With Nico now at the scene, the cops holding Sammy in place, Miles walked over with Vanessa at his side and asked the fake Sammy, "So what about your John Smith who procured all your girls for you? Did you kill him too?"

The guy glared and didn't say a word.

Nico looked at him and supposedly tripped, his foot coming up hard against Sammy's gunshot shoulder, and the man roared with pain. He jumped forward, but Nico then suddenly fell down again and this time landed on his knees, using the guy's shoulder for support. "Oh, God," Nico said. "I'm sorry. This is really rough ground here."

But the man was bent over, twisting up in a fetal position and bawling like a baby.

"Interesting," Nico said, looking down at him. "You know what? You're kind of pathetic. I didn't really think that you'd be so easy to take down. And look at you. You're bawling like a child. Obviously you couldn't kidnap anyone on your own. You *needed* Ambrose to do your dirty work."

He shook his head. "No, no, no," he said. "I need my lawyer. This is police brutality."

"Oh, well, where did you ever get the idea that I'm police?" Nico asked.

Vanessa chuckled. "And you, asshole, I want to know why you were taking me away."

"For my collection," he said.

Everybody around him froze.

"*Your* collection?" Miles asked in a warning tone.

But the guy was too oblivious, the pain curling him up in a tiny and tight ball. He nodded. "Yes. My collection."

"And where is this collection?"

He shrugged.

"Tell us," Nico said, his hand coming down hard on Sammy's injured shoulder.

The man started to blubber, "Please, please no."

"Where is this collection?"

"At home," he said.

"And where's home?"

He gave the name of a small town farther up the coast.

Miles looked down at her, and she said, "Don't even think about it. I'm going with you."

"Are you sure?"

She nodded. "Absolutely sure."

He looked down at the buyer and asked, "And why are you collecting these redheads?"

The man opened his eyes, and they were filled with tears of sorrow this time. "I wouldn't have to," he said, "but they keep wanting to leave me."

"Did you keep them as prisoners?" Vanessa asked brutally.

He nodded slowly.

"You can never cage what needs to be free," she said. "One way or another, they all will find a way to escape, even if it's into death."

And he started to blubber again. "But I loved them," he said. "I would have loved you too. I would have kept you so happy."

"There's no true happiness to be found if you keep

women as prisoners," she said. "And why did you start all this?"

"She died," he said. "That asshole killed her."

At that, Miles understood a few of the puzzle pieces. "So, this John Smith or Ambrose or whatever he liked to be called, killed your girlfriend?"

"No, she was his girlfriend," he said. "She was *my* sister."

"And he killed your sister?"

Vanessa crouched in front of him and reached out to hold his hand.

Immediately Miles tried to pull her back, but she refused. "And you loved her, didn't you?"

He nodded. "I so loved her. She was everything to me."

"And was she your lover?"

He nodded. "We'd been lovers forever," he whispered. "She was older than me, but then she started to see John Smith. And they got into a big fight when he found out that she loved me too."

"And he killed her."

"Yes," he whispered. "He killed her. And I watched him do it, and I couldn't stop him, but, at the same time, I now had power over him. Because he had killed to get even, he realized that killing made him feel good. And so he would kill every once in a while, just enough to stave off the pain. But then he realized that it made him just as happy to pick up women for me."

"But only redheads, right?"

"Yes," he whispered, "Only redheads. And only when I needed them."

"Like once a year."

He shrugged. "Sometimes, I'd have two, if the other one was still alive. Every year in the same month, he'd bring me a new one. I paid him a lot of money to keep quiet and to keep me happy. I have money ..." He looked up at the people surrounding him. But, at the frowns glaring back, he sagged in on himself. "I have money," he whispered. "I created a video game and made enough money to keep my collection happy."

Happy? That was hardly the right word. Miles could feel the growing anger all around him. "You didn't choose them?"

The fake Sammy nodded. "Some of them I did. You, I did," he whispered to Vanessa. "You were so beautiful," he said, staring up at her with longing. "All those photos, all the pictures everywhere ... So beautiful I knew I had to have you."

"There, that possession thing again," she said. "Did you kill all those women?"

He shook his head. "No, of course not. I never killed them."

"Did John?" Miles asked.

Sammy looked at him briefly, but his gaze slid away.

"So, when he brought you a new one every year, you let him kill the old one?" Vanessa asked, her voice rising in horror. "Isn't it bad enough that you kept them prisoner all that time, then you turned around and, instead of giving them their freedom, you let that sadistic killer get them too?"

"We were blood brothers," he said. "Nobody else would understand, but he understood me, and I understood him. Then he messed up and lost you. Then shot a cop because he was mad, and he hadn't found you yet. He had a kid who did our IDs, played with the traffic cams, ran errands, ... but he got caught. So I had to step in. I hated it but ..." He stared at Vanessa. "You're worth it."

"Dear God," she said, looking at Miles, her hand at her mouth. "I'm going to be sick." And she turned and vomited into the deep grass.

Miles gently lifted her and pulled her back. "This man'll go to prison, and we're taking you to the hospital."

She stared at him and nodded slowly. "I still need to know where this John Smith/Ambrose is."

Miles looked down and said to Sammy, "He's back at your prison, isn't he?"

Sammy started to bawl again. "He's my blood brother," he said, "and I killed him."

"Why?" she asked, still struggling to understand.

CHAPTER 13

"WHY DID YOU kill him?" Vanessa asked the fake Sammy.

"Because he failed," he said simply. "I had warned him after the last one. Another failure and I'd kill him myself."

"I'm surprised he didn't kill you," Miles said.

"He tried," Sammy said. "That's why I killed him first. I saw the police rescue once Vanessa escaped. I heard all about it in the news, and then I went to the hospital to stand guard. Ross helped with the fake ID and creating my personnel file with the hospital. And then I went to Vanessa's apartment. Nobody ever questioned me. Nobody ever does. I'm one of those people nobody ever notices twice."

"Well, that's all right," she said. "Now you'll be known as the partner to the worst serial killer in this part of London."

At that, he started to bawl again. "I didn't want to hurt them. They were beautiful. They were just so beautiful, and they were mine."

"Well, they were never yours to begin with," she said.

He looked at her and shook his head. "But he always brought me a shiny new one, and I couldn't resist."

She stared at him in sick disgust and stumbled to the SUV, where she bent down again and took deep breaths.

Her stomach was already pretty upset. When she felt warm arms around her, she turned and curled into Miles's embrace. "Dear God," she whispered.

He stroked her head gently. "I know. I know. Let's get you to the hospital and get your shoulder looked after."

She nodded. "And please make sure we confirm the other asshole is dead."

"We will," he said. "As far as you're concerned, this is over."

"But all those women," she whispered. "And that's such a shitty reason to die, because he got a new one for his collection."

"Any of this is a shitty reason to die," he said. "The good news is, it wasn't your turn."

She smiled up at him and said, "No, not anymore, thanks to you."

"You rescued yourself the first time," he said. "I had to redeem myself and rescue you this time."

She chuckled. "So now you can be Sir Galahad. Get me treated and take me home, please, preferably to bed."

He helped her into the front of the SUV. Then he turned to Nico, still with fake Sammy and the police.

Nico waved him off. "I'm going up to the other house of horrors. I want to make sure that Ambrose is dead."

"Let us know, please." Miles then gently maneuvered the SUV through the throng and headed back toward the hospital. "I suggest we call your sister and let her know you're okay."

"Oh, yes, please."

He pulled out his phone and called the number as she reeled it off again.

When Ruby answered the phone, he put it on Speaker,

and Vanessa cried out, "Ruby?"

And Ruby started to bawl. "Oh, my God," she said. "Please tell me that you're safe."

"I'm safe," she said. "Miles rescued me."

At that, the two women spoke quietly as he drove steadily back toward the heart of London. He took her to the hospital and back into the emergency room, where she was treated right away, with the rest of her wounds checked over and finally bandaged up. He put the painkiller medication in his pocket, and he led her back to her apartment. Ruby was staying with her friends for the night, and Miles didn't plan on leaving Vanessa's side.

When they got to the front steps, he swooped her into his arms, and she chuckled. "You know something? I could get used to this."

"Well, it's certainly not a hardship on my part either," he said. "You could gain a few pounds as far as I'm concerned."

"Not until after my modeling contract is done," she said.

"What about the scar on your shoulder? Will that hurt your career?"

"Nah," she said. "I'll wear that proudly."

Inside her apartment, he set her gently on her feet and took a look around. "Where was he?"

Her lips trembled as she pointed and told Miles exactly what had happened and where fake Sammy had jumped out of the closet at her.

Miles nodded and asked, "Do you want me to check the place?"

She thought about it, then smiled and shook her head. "No, I think we're good now."

"Good for you," he said, "but I'm not taking any chances." And he swept through the entire apartment, checking under the beds and in the closets. When his phone rang a little bit later, he answered to hear Nico confirm that John Smith alias John Ambrose was dead. Smiling, he hung up the phone and walked in to see her lying in bed.

"So, good news," he said. "John Smith aka John Ambrose is also dead. Confirmed by Nico."

She smiled. "Good. So it's over with."

"It is." He sat down on the side of the bed and frowned at her. "How's the pain?"

She smiled and said, "It's terrible. I think you need to kiss it all better."

He murmured gently as he lowered his head. "But then I don't know where I wouldn't have to kiss," he said. "There are so many beautiful areas to touch, to kiss."

She arched up underneath his body, sliding her good arm up and around his neck and said, "Well, you better get started then."

He lifted his head, dropping little kisses on her chin and her lips, and stopped to ask, "Are you sure?"

"I have never been more certain of anything in my life." She tucked him lower and kissed him deeply.

When he pulled his head back, he said, "Wow, you pack a punch, lady."

"Yeah," she said. "I've got a lot of bruises for it." And then she smiled. "Let's celebrate life and leave all that death and nastiness behind."

"That works for me," he whispered, then pulled himself back and quickly stripped down.

She nodded. "Right. And I'm so damn injured it would be a little hard to be sexy while trying to get me undressed."

He laughed. "Sweetie, you'll always be sexy."

But it took a little bit of effort to gently get the clothes off her body without hurting her, and then she stood in front of him, not quite as tall as he was, but definitely thin yet curvy, her breasts just the perfect size for his hands.

He shook his head. "Like I said, you're beautifully gorgeous. Even more so than your photos." He bent down and pulled all the blankets and sheets back, and she laid back down again. "Considering how banged up you are," he said as he waggled his eyebrows, then he leaned down beside her as he laid down on his back. Plus he didn't want to bring up bad old memories of that man from her childhood laying atop her. He'd have to gently work around to that.

She didn't get it for a moment, and then she laughed and rolled over on top with him and said, "You know what? That's a darn good idea." And she gently kissed him.

But he wouldn't just lie there. Instead, his hands stroked like feathers up and down her skin, careful of the bruised areas, her ribs and her sore shoulder.

"Every damn part of me hurts," she moaned. "But I want this so much." And she kissed him and let her tongue tangle with his as she laid on top of him, completely from hip to chest, as his hands gently cupped and caressed the hills and valleys, taking the time to gently raise the passion between them, a passion which was already and always had been just barely banked between them.

When finally shuddering and quaking, she pushed herself up and murmured, "I don't think I can wait."

She raised herself up and then lowered herself slowly on his erection, coming down to seat herself firmly at the base. She arched backward using her good arm, and she grabbed a hold of his leg and pushed herself deeper and deeper against him. She could hear him groaning underneath. Slowly she shifted forward and leaned down, pressing her good arm on his shoulder and started to ride.

He reached up and grasped her hips gently in his hands, holding her so she didn't go too high, and raising his hips up as they found a rhythm between them. And faster and faster, her body naturally picking up the rhythm as they both drove to the cliff edge. Finally she cried out, and he ground up deep and hard against her, his hands holding her hips firm against him, and he joined her over the cliff. She slowly slid down, ignoring the pain as she came down a little too hard on her ribs, and he tucked her up close. "Are you okay?"

"I'm fine," she said. "My ribs are a bit tender."

He kissed her gently and tucked her up into the blankets and said, "You've had painkillers. Maybe just sleep."

"And maybe not," she whispered. "I feel like every time I turn around, I get knocked unconscious, and I'm forced into sleep. I don't want to sleep right now. Just remind me of all the good things in life."

"I could tell you how I fell in love with you the very first time I saw your photo in the swimsuit issue of a magazine."

She laughed, a happy sound that reverberated in his heart. "When was this?"

"About ten years ago."

"Wow. I had just landed my first big modeling gig."

"And you are even more beautiful now."

"Wow. You can talk to me about the good things in my life any time you want to," she said with a happy sigh, her breathing slowing down more and more.

He leaned over and kissed her gently. "We have a lifetime for that," he said. "There's no rush."

"Promise?" she whispered.

He nodded. "I promise." And he gently drew the sheet

up over her body, then rearranged it so that she was tucked up against him spoon style and held her close.

"I'm really glad that you rescued me," she whispered.

"Me too," he said. "You aren't the only one who'll have nightmares."

She laced her fingers between his and held him close, then whispered, "That's okay. I'll be here to hold you through the worst of them."

He smiled and whispered against her ear, "Ditto."

She chuckled, and her eyes drifted closed. And, caught up in the circle of love and in his arms, she fell asleep once again.

EPILOGUE

NICO WALKED AWAY from the house of horrors, feeling something sickening growing inside him and trying to retch outward. He rarely got sick on a job, but, man, seeing the prison where those poor women had been kept and seeing how wretched their lives had been just made Nico seriously ill. He had a quiet sense of satisfaction though for finally closing a case that had tormented him for years. But the way it had closed, … it was beyond painful. He desperately wanted everyone to have a happy ending, and, in a way, because both Vanessa and Ruby were fine, he got one here, but he wanted to kill that bastard over and over again for the useless deaths of the other sixteen redheads.

When his phone rang, he looked down to see it was one of the Mavericks calling.

"Don't even begin to ask me to do a job right now," he said. "I'm quietly being sick in the back yard."

"I'm sorry," Miles said. "That was a rough one, wasn't it?"

"Yeah, it was. These assholes needed to be stopped. At least we finally got them."

"Well, you give me a call when you're ready because I've got another asshole who needs to be stopped."

"Is it as shitty as this one?"

Miles sighed. "It could be much worse, so call me when

you're ready."

NICO STRATUS STARED at his phone in disbelief. A message from Miles. He was half-expecting it, but, at the same time hadn't *really* been expecting it. It was one of those things that he knew was coming, yet he just didn't know when. But it had been days ago that he'd expected it, and, when it didn't come, he'd relaxed. The timing was really crappy right now. He had groceries in a shopping cart in front of him, and he was still halfway through the list in his hand. But then he hadn't been planning on buying very much. Still, it was too much. The message from Miles was clear.

Leave now.

Swearing softly, he walked away from his shopping cart, knowing that's the last thing that he would normally do. He shrugged, not having much choice. When he got outside to his car, a nine-by-thirteen brown envelope sat on the front seat. He snatched it up, read the cover note atop the file folder with one burner phone inside and realized he was flying to Australia to a military air base. He swore at that because that would be an all-day trip with a time change to adjust to as well. He drove home quickly and parked his vehicle in the underground parking, then walked up to his apartment and snagged his to-go bags. He did a check to make sure everything had been replenished since his last op before he turned and walked back out again. He had no idea when he'd be back. He was currently living in San Diego and close to Coronado's military base. That meant a fast flight out.

As he hopped into the waiting cab—courtesy of Miles

and the Mavericks—and was driven to the airport, Nico studied the files in the folder. His itinerary was there as well as a dossier. He stared at it and shook his head, whispering, "Why the hell am I even going for something like this?"

Just then his new burner phone beeped, and a series of texts rolled through.

Parcel waiting for you at the airport. More burner phones. All communication to be silent.

He quickly texted back. **Does anybody know I'll be there?**

Only your partner, who you will meet over there.

And the Australian government is okay with this?

Not likely but they don't know. And we're not telling them at this time. If we can keep it secret, we need to.

Seriously?

Yes. This issue has layers that you don't know about. We need this to be a total blacked-out version of black ops. You'll get all the help you need otherwise.

And the Australian police aren't handling this why? No need for them to know the layers either. And just what kind of case is this?

A woman has gone missing. She's a prominent figure as an activist.

Great. No lack of suspects then. He shook his head. **And the problem here again is?**

Charlotte was over there for a big rally in support of the indigenous people and their problems, injustices in face of the climate issues. She was supposed to give a big speech. Only she wasn't there to give the speech.

And she just disappeared?

From her hotel room, yes.

And she's been reported as a missing person?

Yes, and the police are on it.

He waited because, of course, if the police were still looking for Charlotte, why was Nico called in?

And? He finally typed in exasperation when there was no answer. He looked around to see that they were maybe ten minutes away from the airport.

His phone beeped again, and the text read, **She's the sister of somebody high up in the government who is undercover at the moment.**

"So then I'm sure the Australian government and the local police authorities will be happy to cooperate," he muttered to himself.

But the next text came. **And it's also secret.**

Shit. So I can't ask for help?

Not from the regular channels. The American government has already expressed concern with the Australian government, and everybody is open and cooperating ... but ...

But this is specialized?

Very. They have their own black-op operatives.

Ransom demand?

Not yet. We have very little information on our own.

Do we have any clue to where she's being kept and why her?

It could be because of her high public outburst against the treatment of the indigenous people in Australia.

Oh. That could do it.

Possibly, but then she's been fairly outspoken for a long time, Miles texted. **She's an anthropologist working around the world to promote better treatment for the original people of every country. And it just happens to be Australia that she's in now.**

Is she the activist author who's been in the news a

lot? Nico asked.

Yes, that's her. What we're really concerned about is that our man's been compromised, and she's been taken for him.

This concludes Book 7 of The Mavericks: Miles.
Read about Nico: The Mavericks, Book 8

The Mavericks: Nico (Book #8)

What happens when the very men—trained to make the hard decisions—come up against the rules and regulations that hold them back from doing what needs to be done? They either stay and work within the constraints given to them or they walk away. Only now, for a select few, they have another option:

The Mavericks. A covert black ops team that steps up and break all the rules … but gets the job done.

Welcome to a new military romance series by *USA Today* best-selling author Dale Mayer. A series where you meet new friends and just might get to meet old ones too in this raw and compelling look at the men who keep us safe every day from the darkness where they operate—and live—in the shadows … until someone special helps them step into the light.

With barely enough time to recover from helping out Miles in London, Nico is off to Australia … and a secret mission involving a US covert operative …

When an American undercover operative's sister goes missing in Australia, Nico has to find out if this is connected to the operative or to the sister's own activist background. Apparently she made enemies easily.

Charlotte hadn't wanted to make this trip in the first place, preferring to communicate her polarizing messages through writing her books now. But, bowing under pressure, she finally arrives in Australia, only to be attacked within minutes of reaching her hotel room for the night. After her rescue, she's forced to dig deep into her family and public life to find the mastermind kidnapper and to stay safe as the bodies pile up.

Nothing makes sense in this twisted mission, but Nico is determined to keep Charlotte safe, even as things take a more personal turn …

Find book 8 here!
To find out more visit Dale Mayer's website.
https://geni.us/DMNicoUniversal

Author's Note

Thank you for reading Miles: The Mavericks, Book 7! If you enjoyed the book, please take a moment and leave a short review.

Dear reader,

I love to hear from readers, and you can contact me at my website: www.dalemayer.com or at my Facebook author page. To be informed of new releases and special offers, sign up for my newsletter or follow me on BookBub. And if you are interested in joining Dale Mayer's Reader Group, here is the Facebook sign up page.
http://geni.us/DaleMayerFBGroup

Cheers,
Dale Mayer

About the Author

Dale Mayer is a *USA Today* best-selling author, best known for her SEALs military romances, her Psychic Visions series, and her Lovely Lethal Garden cozy series. Her contemporary romances are raw and full of passion and emotion (Broken But ... Mending, Hathaway House series). Her thrillers will keep you guessing (Kate Morgan, By Death series), and her romantic comedies will keep you giggling (*It's a Dog's Life*, a stand-alone novella; and the Broken Protocols series, starring Charming Marvin, the cat).

Dale honors the stories that come to her—and some of them are crazy, break all the rules and cross multiple genres!

To go with her fiction, she also writes nonfiction in many different fields, with books available on résumé writing, companion gardening, and the US mortgage system. All her books are available in print and ebook format.

Connect with Dale Mayer Online

Dale's Website – www.dalemayer.com

Twitter – @DaleMayer

Facebook Page – geni.us/DaleMayerFBFanPage

Facebook Group – geni.us/DaleMayerFBGroup

BookBub – geni.us/DaleMayerBookbub

Instagram – geni.us/DaleMayerInstagram

Goodreads – geni.us/DaleMayerGoodreads

Newsletter – geni.us/DaleNews

Also by Dale Mayer

Published Adult Books:

Hathaway House

Aaron, Book 1

Brock, Book 2

Cole, Book 3

Denton, Book 4

Elliot, Book 5

Finn, Book 6

Gregory, Book 7

The K9 Files

Ethan, Book 1

Pierce, Book 2

Zane, Book 3

Blaze, Book 4

Lucas, Book 5

Parker, Book 6

Carter, Book 7

Lovely Lethal Gardens

Arsenic in the Azaleas, Book 1

Bones in the Begonias, Book 2

Corpse in the Carnations, Book 3

Daggers in the Dahlias, Book 4

Evidence in the Echinacea, Book 5

Footprints in the Ferns, Book 6

Gun in the Gardenias, Book 7
Handcuffs in the Heather, Book 8

Psychic Vision Series
Tuesday's Child
Hide 'n Go Seek
Maddy's Floor
Garden of Sorrow
Knock Knock…
Rare Find
Eyes to the Soul
Now You See Her
Shattered
Into the Abyss
Seeds of Malice
Eye of the Falcon
Itsy-Bitsy Spider
Unmasked
Deep Beneath
From the Ashes
Psychic Visions Books 1–3
Psychic Visions Books 4–6
Psychic Visions Books 7–9

By Death Series
Touched by Death
Haunted by Death
Chilled by Death
By Death Books 1–3

Broken Protocols – Romantic Comedy Series
Cat's Meow
Cat's Pajamas

Cat's Cradle

Cat's Claus

Broken Protocols 1-4

Broken and... Mending

Skin

Scars

Scales (of Justice)

Broken but... Mending 1-3

Glory

Genesis

Tori

Celeste

Glory Trilogy

Biker Blues

Morgan: Biker Blues, Volume 1

Cash: Biker Blues, Volume 2

SEALs of Honor

Mason: SEALs of Honor, Book 1

Hawk: SEALs of Honor, Book 2

Dane: SEALs of Honor, Book 3

Swede: SEALs of Honor, Book 4

Shadow: SEALs of Honor, Book 5

Cooper: SEALs of Honor, Book 6

Markus: SEALs of Honor, Book 7

Evan: SEALs of Honor, Book 8

Mason's Wish: SEALs of Honor, Book 9

Chase: SEALs of Honor, Book 10

Brett: SEALs of Honor, Book 11

Devlin: SEALs of Honor, Book 12

Easton: SEALs of Honor, Book 13
Ryder: SEALs of Honor, Book 14
Macklin: SEALs of Honor, Book 15
Corey: SEALs of Honor, Book 16
Warrick: SEALs of Honor, Book 17
Tanner: SEALs of Honor, Book 18
Jackson: SEALs of Honor, Book 19
Kanen: SEALs of Honor, Book 20
Nelson: SEALs of Honor, Book 21
Taylor: SEALs of Honor, Book 22
SEALs of Honor, Books 1–3
SEALs of Honor, Books 4–6
SEALs of Honor, Books 7–10
SEALs of Honor, Books 11–13
SEALs of Honor, Books 14–16
SEALs of Honor, Books 17–19

Heroes for Hire

Levi's Legend: Heroes for Hire, Book 1
Stone's Surrender: Heroes for Hire, Book 2
Merk's Mistake: Heroes for Hire, Book 3
Rhodes's Reward: Heroes for Hire, Book 4
Flynn's Firecracker: Heroes for Hire, Book 5
Logan's Light: Heroes for Hire, Book 6
Harrison's Heart: Heroes for Hire, Book 7
Saul's Sweetheart: Heroes for Hire, Book 8
Dakota's Delight: Heroes for Hire, Book 9
Michael's Mercy (Part of Sleeper SEAL Series)
Tyson's Treasure: Heroes for Hire, Book 10
Jace's Jewel: Heroes for Hire, Book 11
Rory's Rose: Heroes for Hire, Book 12
Brandon's Bliss: Heroes for Hire, Book 13

Liam's Lily: Heroes for Hire, Book 14
North's Nikki: Heroes for Hire, Book 15
Anders's Angel: Heroes for Hire, Book 16
Reyes's Raina: Heroes for Hire, Book 17
Dezi's Diamond: Heroes for Hire, Book 18
Vince's Vixen: Heroes for Hire, Book 19
Ice's Icing: Heroes for Hire, Book 20
Heroes for Hire, Books 1–3
Heroes for Hire, Books 4–6
Heroes for Hire, Books 7–9
Heroes for Hire, Books 10–12
Heroes for Hire, Books 13–15

SEALs of Steel

Badger: SEALs of Steel, Book 1
Erick: SEALs of Steel, Book 2
Cade: SEALs of Steel, Book 3
Talon: SEALs of Steel, Book 4
Laszlo: SEALs of Steel, Book 5
Geir: SEALs of Steel, Book 6
Jager: SEALs of Steel, Book 7
The Final Reveal: SEALs of Steel, Book 8
SEALs of Steel, Books 1–4
SEALs of Steel, Books 5–8
SEALs of Steel, Books 1–8

The Mavericks

Kerrick, Book 1
Griffin, Book 2
Jax, Book 3
Beau, Book 4
Asher, Book 5
Ryker, Book 6

Miles, Book 7
Nico, Book 8
Keane, Book 9
Lennox, Book 10
Gavin, Book 11
Shane, Book 12

Collections
Dare to Be You…
Dare to Love…
Dare to be Strong…
RomanceX3

Standalone Novellas
It's a Dog's Life
Riana's Revenge
Second Chances

Published Young Adult Books:

Family Blood Ties Series
Vampire in Denial
Vampire in Distress
Vampire in Design
Vampire in Deceit
Vampire in Defiance
Vampire in Conflict
Vampire in Chaos
Vampire in Crisis
Vampire in Control
Vampire in Charge
Family Blood Ties Set 1–3
Family Blood Ties Set 1–5

Family Blood Ties Set 4–6
Family Blood Ties Set 7–9
Sian's Solution, A Family Blood Ties Series Prequel
    Novelette

Design series
Dangerous Designs
Deadly Designs
Darkest Designs
Design Series Trilogy

Standalone
In Cassie's Corner
Gem Stone (a Gemma Stone Mystery)
Time Thieves

Published Non-Fiction Books:

Career Essentials
Career Essentials: The Résumé
Career Essentials: The Cover Letter
Career Essentials: The Interview
Career Essentials: 3 in 1